Death Benefits

by

Sharon Saracino

Max Logan Series, Book 1

Death Benefits

Cover Art by *Debbie Taylor*

The Wild Rose Press, Inc.
PO Box 708
Adams Basin, NY 14410-0708
Visit us at www.thewildrosepress.com

Publishing History
First Fantasy Rose Edition, 2016
Print ISBN 978-1-5092-0845-6
Digital ISBN 978-1-5092-0846-3

Max Logan Series, Book 1
Published in the United States of America

I could not be dead.

I was only thirty-five years old and in excellent health, for a dead chick. I still had things to do, places to go, people to see. And I planned to, just as soon as I got the motivation to leave my apartment. I closed my eyes and clicked my heels three times. I wiggled my nose. I wished on a falling star. If Marvin wasn't hogging the keyboard, I would have hit Ctrl+Alt+Del. I took a deep breath and opened my eyes. Nothing had changed.

"That's impossible," I said in a flat voice that sounded far calmer than you would expect under the circumstances. "I'm not in your database. Obviously there's been a mistake. Just send me back and we'll call it even. It'll be our little secret." Elizabeth Kubler-Ross documented five stages of grieving. Other authorities have identified up to seven. But, no matter which theory you subscribe to, all have one thing in common: the first stage is denial. I planned to keep my butt firmly planted in stage one, Denial with a capital D.

Praise for Sharon Saracino

The Max Logan Series—2015 Paranormal Romance Guild Reviewers' Choice Nominee for Best Paranormal Series

~*~

"With tremendous humor and a sharp wit, Sharon Saracino offers a look at what soul searching is all about…"

~Readers' Favorite Book Reviews

~*~

"Witty, insightful, and frequently hilarious, Saracino's writing keeps me up late into the night, chuckling and cheering into my blankets. This series has quickly become one of my favorite reads!"

~AJ Nuest, author of She's Got Dibs

Dedication

In Loving Memory
For Mom
No matter how many lessons Max learns in death,
they can't compare to the lessons you taught me in life.
I miss you every day.

Acknowledgments

Thank you to my family and friends for their support and encouragement, especially my sister Kathy Fino and my forever friend Gwen Nakao, both of whom listen endlessly, encourage unconditionally, and still answer the phone every time I call. With equal parts gratitude and admiration, I thank the many fellow writers who gave so generously of their time, talents, and experience, especially John Fraser Williams who inspired me to dust off my pen after years of neglect and Susan Meier who taught me the tools.

Thank you to my son Vincent, who makes me laugh and worry in equal measure, who forces me to think outside the box, and who often leaves me stunned with the realization that I actually gave birth to this bright and talented being.

And finally, thank you to my husband Vince, who takes care of absolutely everything else, so that I can do the things I love. His love and support are infinite and there aren't enough words to express my gratitude. You are my heart.

Chapter One

Stupid way to die? Been there, done that. Who says death can't be funny? Even I can admit it isn't the most auspicious way to start the weekend. Karma is so arbitrary.

The day I died began uneventfully enough, remarkable only for the unprovoked and unexpected attack launched by a slick-faced teen with a slippery façade of moderate acne and purple braces at the SuperSave checkout, of all places. I put my righteous indignation on hold long enough to wonder when good old fashioned tinsel teeth, inducing untold nights of teenage angst and lifelong psychological consequences, had been replaced by a psychedelic fashion statement stretched between misshapen molars.

He eyed me politely over the top of his Coke bottle-thick Buddy Holly specs, one grimy-nailed finger poised over the register key, and fired the opening volley. *"Will that be all, ma'am?"*

Just like that. I swore I heard a bell toll somewhere. *Ma'am*: the moniker that had been heretofore reserved for my stepmother and others of her geriatric generation. I surreptitiously eyed the other shoppers waiting in line. Not one of them appeared the least bit outraged on my behalf. Desperately clinging to the coattails of youth with ragged and bloodied fingernails, I felt myself sliding slowly down the slippery slope of a rut, forced to acknowledge perhaps the battle had ended and I was left alone, completely unarmed.

It should not have been an epiphany.

Oh sure, I'd noticed the stranger staring back at me in the mirror over my toothbrush every morning. *She* had slowly been acquiring fine lines, a few extra pounds, and an insidiously increasing reliance on foundation garments. Most days, I refused to acknowledge *she* bore any resemblance to me. Each morning, I rejoiced when I stepped on the scale and weighed exactly the same as I did in high school, until *she* put my other foot on the scale. *She* and I existed in two different decades. The decades were not consecutive.

In case you were wondering, rationalization is an acquired talent. I could probably give workshops.

I lifted my chin and stared down my nose at 'Buddy,' the cashier, in what I hoped was a mature and intimidating manner. What I really wanted to do was, well…slap him. Hard. My bifocals were buried in the lost world of my handbag, and squinting to read the name embroidered in white on his red polyester vest might have ruined the menacing effect I intended. As far as I could tell, Buddy remained totally oblivious to the implied threat. He simply regarded me with a sad and thoughtful look as I attempted to unobtrusively rearrange a loaf of whole wheat bread on the top of my eco-friendly tote, the better to camouflage my moisturizer, chocolate sandwich cookies with double stuff, and the box of rich brown number 57A hair coloring, because, damn it, I *am* worth it.

I haughtily stalked past the bag boy after swiping my debit card, punching in my PIN, and poking the "accept" button with a little more force than may have been strictly necessary. My irritation was totally wasted on Brace Face and Bag Boy who had already refocused their hormone induced adolescent attention on the three barely pubescent titterers—pun intended—who were racking brains even smaller than their short shorts over the monumental decision of whether to buy cinnamon or spearmint breath mints. Ah, kids…our hope for the future. It gave me the warm fuzzies, especially when I theorized someone of my apparently advanced years would be unlikely to reap the benefit of their questionably mature wisdom, if and when they ever acquired any.

As for me, I felt as though Scotty had already flicked the switch to beam-me-up, and left me helplessly cavorting in space somewhere between the Starship Thirty-something and the planet Middle Age. Whoever coined the catchphrase that fifty is the new thirty did so while blowing out forty-nine birthday candles and scrambling desperately away from the precipice of the half-century abyss.

I schlepped listlessly through the parking lot, vaguely annoyed at the way my lime green flip-flops kept sticking to the half melted tar lines dissecting the broiling asphalt. I loaded my bags into the trunk, my body enveloped in an intimate embrace of thick, humid, air. I tried to enjoy it, as it was the closest thing I'd had to an intimate embrace in quite a while.

I'd left the car windows open, but the impact was negligible, and I winced at the hot sting of burning vinyl sticking to my thighs when I climbed in, hoping it might magically melt some of the unsightly cellulite I'd noticed of late. I concentrated on taking shallow breaths, the better to avoid asphyxiation in the overheated interior of the car, and cranked the fan up to the highest speed. The vents blasted air as stale and refreshing as something channeled straight from the furnaces of hell, accompanied by a faint tang of stale nicotine, my own personal brimstone.

I knew it would be at least ten minutes before the AC kicked in enough to make my ride tolerable. Of course, by then I would be home. I pressed a hand to my chest irritably, drowning the front of my already moist, blue tank top in the river running wild between my breasts.

Have I mentioned I don't do temperature extremes?

My mood had no cause to improve on the drive home as I considered the vacuum that had become my everyday existence: divorced, depressed, unemployed, but according to my former therapist, only slightly delusional. Yay, me! Some days I was okay with my life. I mean, things could always get better, right? Other days the perceived injustice of it all kicked my butt. Guess which way I was swinging today? Flight FU2 to my happy place took a fatal nosedive as I started to pull into the gravel drive of my apartment, which coincidentally was situated on the second story of my father's detached garage.

Location, location, location. I know, right?

I wrenched the wheel back toward the street, narrowly avoiding the sparkling, cobalt blue X5 luxury SUV blocking the entrance to the drive. The gleaming, chrome grill positively leered at me as I parked at the curb and awkwardly heaved my bags across the yard and up the stairs from the street. The Golden Child, aka my half-sister Denise, was apparently in residence. I suppose when you are the axis around which the world revolves, it doesn't enter your mind someone else might need a place to park. Catty? Maybe. But, these days, if it weren't for mood swings, I'm not sure I would get any exercise at all.

Denise is a tall, willowy blonde with the face of an angel, the fashion sense of a supermodel, and a shoe collection to rival Imelda Marcos'. Me? Not so much. Next to Denise, I usually came off feeling like a small, dark troll. Is it any wonder I preferred to revel in the joys of my solitary apartment? People say I'm insecure. I prefer to think I'm just realistic about my limitations. My steer-clear-of-the-family plan bit the dust as soon as my stepmother spotted me leaning on the banister, panting. I immediately regretted I hadn't simply soldiered on instead of stopping on the landing to catch my breath and pray for deliverance from heatstroke.

"Yoo-hoo, Maxine! Denise is here," she called with her usual uncanny flair for redundancy.

As if anyone could miss the two thousand pound display of sparkling soccer mom extravagance crouched like a gargoyle at the end of the drive? Lacking adequate oxygen to verbalize a response, I briefly considered waving to Captain Obvious in recognition of her pointless announcement before realizing my arms had, in fact, gone numb from the weight of the bags, compounded by the distance of my hike from the street. Thank God I'd only needed a couple of things. I settled for jerking my chin in some spasmodic seizure-like acknowledgment and hoped Gail was able to see it from the window. Bracing myself against the inevitable leg cramps sure to assault me when I finally reached the top, I huffed up the remaining stairs and stepped inside with a groan, kicking the door closed behind me. It was a religious experience. There is a God, and thou shall call him Central Air.

I dumped the bags onto the black, marble-topped island alternately serving as my kitchen counter-office-fine dining area, depending upon the occasion. My galley kitchen, a modern, sleek, state of the art affair of stainless steel efficiency, occupied the right wall. At least I assumed it would be efficient, if I used it.

The main room was spacious and airy with a bank of windows along the back, and French doors which opened onto a small deck covered with a red striped awning. Very French bistro. At least it had been until I replaced the dainty iron chairs with old, hulking Adirondacks. They're really more my style. There was a separate, but equally spacious bedroom with an attached bath, in addition to a compact, but tastefully decorated guest powder room off of the living area.

Guests? Hey, it could happen.

The bathroom fixtures and kitchen appliances were new, but the furniture was not. I estimated it was produced somewhere in the era between truly antique and fashionably dumpster worthy. Not that I'd expected Gail to spend a fortune refurbishing the place.

After all, I was only the inconvenient stepdaughter, turning up again like a bad penny, right? But even with the older stuff, I had to admit the woman had flair, and while I'd never admit it to her, the decor suited me. There was something familiar and comforting about it at a time when I needed comfort and familiarity more than almost anything. Sure, the apartment was an OBOG (one bedroom over garage), but when that garage was a five bay, it made for over a thousand square feet of airy, bachelorette breathing room, and it was all mine. Sort of. Well, for as long as I needed it, anyway. Luckily for me, my father is a car junkie.

I absently marched in place, slapping at my thighs and kneading my calves until the circulation in my legs resumed a normal, relatively pain-free flow. Maybe Denise's husband, Brad-The-Famous-Vascular-Surgeon, was right and my leg cramps were a result of intermittent claudication. Brad-The-Famous-Vascular-Surgeon never missed an opportunity to explain my discomfort on stairs was due, no doubt, to peripheral arterial disease, implying significant atherosclerotic blockages in the blood vessels of my legs, the only outcome a woman of my advancing age, questionable diet, and the half a pack a day habit I periodically tried to kick, could realistically expect.

Yeah, those were his exact words. Such a charmer, is our Brad—assuming you are using a thesaurus listing charmer and pompous ass as synonyms. But he does put up with my high maintenance sister, so maybe he does have some redeeming quality buried beneath his argyle sweaters and cashmere socks. The socks are black. He wears them every day, all year long. Even in the summer. With sandals.

It is not an attractive look. Just saying.

My sister and her husband are an oddly mismatched couple, but despite my opinion, which no one asked for, as usual, they seem surprisingly happy together. At least I could look forward to a family discount on the fem-pop bypass he so clearly envisioned in my future. Denise's marriage to Brad-

The-Famous-Vascular-Surgeon was Stepmother Gail's claim to Red Hat Society celebrity.

Of course, as a dutiful step-daughter, I'd done my part to help Gail attain her elevated status by first marrying a doctor, myself. We're divorced now. The last time I checked, he was dating Barbara-The-Blonde-Bimbo-With-Implants. Body like a goddess, brain like a brick—at least that's my theory. Sure, I'd noticed Roger had become a little distant, but I figured it was one of those phases a marriage goes through.

Until the fateful night at Alberto's when I walked in and found the two of them huddled in a booth. Business meeting, yeah right. For a while, I worried I might become bitter, but thank God I managed to nip it in the bud. I've since decided it's only right to pass along my playthings to the less fortunate when I have no further use for them. I will admit that beyond the obvious draw, which I like to call Thing One and Thing Two, I've never understood Roger's interest in Barbie. Even I can admit Roger is brilliant. I have to wonder what they talk about. Of course, maybe they've found something to do that doesn't involve intelligent conversation, but I'd rather not look at that too closely, if you don't mind. Yes, Roger-The-Proctologist certainly chose an appropriate specialty in the end. Turns out he is a professional asshole.

Roger had vacated our marriage with the condo, the vintage classic car, and the time share in Nassau. I'd gotten my ten year old jalopy and the cat. I figured I'd come out ahead since Caesar was far better company, and the car required significantly less maintenance, than Roger-The-Proctologist did. And my alimony turned out to be a nice chunk of change, which is fortunate since it is pretty much my only income at the moment. Rumor has it, not that I pay attention to such things—much—that Barbara-The-Blonde-Bimbo-With-Implants eventually assumed another of my former positions as Roger's Office Manager. Of course, Roger never asked me to leave, it just became too difficult to stay. And at least I gave him a two-week notice, which is more than he gave me. My philosophy is that Barbie isn't too bright, but apparently she is quite flexible, in ways I honestly don't care to contemplate. Roger periodically tries to renegotiate my monthly remuneration. He argues it's already too much. I usually shut him up by arguing what's actually too much is the two gallons of saline bobbling around on Barbara-The-Blonde-Bimbo-With-Implants' chest. Frankly, I think she overpaid. Twenty grand is a bit steep for two heavy duty balloons filled with saltwater when you come right down to it.

It was unseasonably hot, even for June, and I gifted myself with a few more minutes of familial avoidance to swipe a cold washcloth over the sweat gelling on the back of my neck since it was clear my repeat shower was not happening anytime soon. My cat, Sir Chicken Caesar, wove a graceful—well, as graceful as a twenty-two pound cat can manage—acrobatic figure eight around my ankles, hinting he'd like to check out the grocery bags.

Yeah, well, how did you think he got to be twenty-two pounds?

I stashed my groceries, left my box of hair coloring on the counter to take into the bathroom later, and dumped a can of tuna surprise in Caesar's blue pottery bowl with the little white paw prints around the side. I love my cat, but I draw the line at using a crystal parfait goblet like they do on those cat food commercials. First of all, I don't own one, and secondly, neither Caesar nor I are that pretentious. And frankly, I could ding a fork against the glass all day long, Caesar doesn't come until he's good and ready.

I concluded my poor, soggy shirt already looked like it had had the crap kicked out of it, so I ran the washcloth over my neck and chest once more and pulled on a loose, white tee announcing "I'm Having One of Those Decades". When at last I could stall no longer—well, okay, I could. In fact if procrastination were a sport, I would be an Olympic gold medalist—I marched downstairs, sans leg cramps, and let myself in the back door of my father's house.

I was immediately slapped in the head, and nearly sent into respiratory arrest, by the overpowering aroma of chocolate hazelnut coffee. Denise had recently gotten Gail one of those nifty little coffee makers that brews individual cups and the two of them were determined to try every last flavor, even when it was approaching a hundred degrees outside.

Of course, I didn't have much room to talk. In my humble opinion there were only two things a girl could never have enough of—caffeine and moisturizer. Followed closely by carbohydrates in any form, and, of course, sleep, the more, the better. I looked at the shiny, chrome carousel holding an impressive selection of the little individual serving cartridges and gave it an experimental spin. As I expected, not only were the cups sorted by flavor, color, and caffeine content, each label was also perfectly aligned with the one next to it. Gail had a tendency to be a little OCD.

I grabbed a heavy, green earthenware mug from the

cabinet and popped in a little cartridge of double espresso. The unrelenting heat might be sucking me dry, but I was suddenly feeling like I could use a boost. In seconds I had a steaming, fragrant eight ounce portion of nirvana. I added a hefty dollop of heavy cream from the fridge and stirred briskly. Sip, swallow, repeat. Thus fortified, I felt ready to face the blonde battalion. Before leaving the kitchen, I twisted the entire collection of cartridges in their holders so the labels went in different directions. I take my cheap thrills where I find them. Sue me.

As it was only mid-afternoon, I knew my father was still downtown at Logan's Hardware, source of the family's bread, butter, and five car garage. Hamilton was still small enough that the nearest large home improvement stores were at least twenty miles away, so the big guy did okay, even in the struggling economy.

I found Gail and Denise at the dining room table, flavored coffee cooling at their elbows, and golden heads bent close together over a pile of House Divine magazines. Apparently, Denise was redecorating. Again. I guess she got that from her mother. Almost as soon as she had a ring on her finger, Stepmother Gail had started working to eradicate every vestige of my mother from the family home. As an adult, I could appreciate her need to put her own stamp on the place, but as an eight year old, it simply pissed me off. As for Denise, she changed her décor as often as some people changed their underwear. She thought it made her appear hip. I thought it made her appear indecisive. I love my sister, but personally, I was pretty sure she could have a far greater impact on beautifying the world if she would just concentrate on redecorating

Brad-The-Famous-Vascular-Surgeon's sock drawer. I have, in fact, suggested it.

"Hey, Max," Denise waved me over. "What do you think of this sofa?" I set my cup on the corner of the gleaming, mahogany table, deliberately ignoring the coaster, and glanced over her shoulder at the slick, glossy layout.

"Denise, didn't you have a sofa exactly like that about five years ago?" Denise, in her usual selectively obtuse fashion, missed the sarcasm completely and drew her finely arched and professionally waxed brows together in thought.

"No, I don't think so?"

I slumped into the chair across from her and wrapped my lips around the rim of my mug to hide a smirk. "My mistake. It's pretty. I think you should definitely consider it."

"Well…actually, I was thinking it would look really great in your place. Maybe with a couple of club chairs and some cool pillows…"

I set my mug down hurriedly as Gail pointedly shoved a coaster beneath it. "Forget it, Sis. I'm quite comfortable with my place exactly the way it is."

"But, Max," Denise cajoled. "You've been living over there for what? Over a year? You haven't changed a thing since you moved in. Change is good!" Well, I can't say I've personally found that to be the case, but then again, unlike Denise, I am not the Charmed One.

"Sure I did, I changed the deck chairs. Look, Denise, I appreciate the thought, honestly…but first of all, I still haven't found a job, so redecorating isn't a priority, and besides, I like my place. It's comfortable, it's predictable, and it's me."

"You know Dad would be happy to hire you down at the store until you find something you prefer."

"I know, but I'm already living here. I can't depend on my father for everything."

Denise sighed and flipped the magazine closed with a snap. She tossed her straight, pale hair over her shoulders. Have I mentioned my half-sister and I look nothing alike? I'm as small, curvy, and dark, as Denise is tall, slim, and blonde. My hair is thick and wavy, hers is baby fine and poker straight. Even in shorts and a T-shirt she managed to look like she just walked out of a magazine. People rarely believe we're related. And that's even before I open my mouth.

Fact number one about me? These days, there is about a ninety-nine percent chance if there is a thought in my head, it will be exiting through my mouth. So to anyone who is offended…I'm working on it. Honest. I try hard, but occasionally, I slip. I guess you could say I've gained a reputation as a bit of a smart-ass. It's not deliberate. Sometimes things unfortunately have a tendency to exit my lips before my brain is able to decide if it's the wisest course of action. Actually, I'm pretty sure I only say what other people are thinking but are too polite to articulate. My father and Denise see the occasional humor. Stepmother Gail? Not so much. I've reconciled myself to the fact I'll never be the perfection that is Denise. Sometimes it hurts, but mostly I'm okay with being the black sheep. Black is slimming.

Now that I'd gone and spoiled Denise's fun, she turned to her mother with a wide-eyed pout.

"You talk to her, Mother. I could do so much with the place, you know. If it's the money, Max, well, maybe you could consider it an early birthday gift."

Since it was ten months until my next birthday, she might be pushing the envelope on that one. I suspect that buying and spending is Denise's way of showing affection. Judging by the fifteen-hundred count Egyptian cotton bed linens she got me for my last birthday, she must really love me. I could have eaten for a month on what they cost.

"Leave it alone, Denise," Gail put in quietly. "I know you mean well, and I'm sure your sister knows, too. But really, honey, sometimes you go a bit too far. Maybe the reason Max doesn't want a change has nothing to do with money. It's her home and she can do whatever she wants with it."

I was relatively sure my eyebrows had completely disappeared into my hairline. I turned to regard my stepmother and did a quick perusal for hidden cameras. I listened for the Twilight Zone theme song playing in the background. I waited for Ashton Kutcher to jump out and tell me I'd been Punked. My stepmother was taking my part over Denise's? Maybe I'd stumbled into an amateur production of Invasion of the Body Snatchers. I might have assumed I'd misheard, but Denise appeared equally surprised to be thus reprimanded. It was a whole new look on her and I bit my lip, hard, to keep from remarking on it.

See, I can show restraint.

"Um…thanks, Gail."

My stepmother shrugged uncomfortably, not meeting my eyes. She rose from the chair and began to gather and stack the magazines, alphabetizing as she went along. "I often wish I'd kept more of my own mother's things," she said even more quietly.

Her mother's things? What was she talking about?

When the realization came, it hit me like a giant mudslide. My apartment. The mismatched, not so new furniture. Gail hadn't decorated my place in second-hand chic, she'd kept my mother's things stored away all these years. For me. She'd never mentioned it, never attempted to take any credit for it. No wonder everything had felt so familiar and comfortable. And until this moment, I hadn't even realized it. Or appreciated it. Or thanked her for it.

My bad.

"Well, I've gotta run. Soccer practice will be over soon, and the girls will be starving."

The girls were my nieces, seven year old twins, Michaela and Victoria. Before you go giving Denise credit for not choosing two of those cutesy rhyming sound-alike names for her twin bundles of joy, you should be aware those two elegant and sophisticated names had been reduced, almost since birth, to Micki and Vicki.

Denise might still be a little put out about the sofa, but she had recovered her composure and conceded the battle. She dropped a kiss on her mother's cheek and gave me a quick hug. "I'll call you later, Mom." Before either Stepmother Gail or I could formulate a response, Denise was out the door in a flash of butterscotch blonde, red soled pumps, and rhinestone studded sunglasses, leaving a moderately uncomfortable silence in her wake.

Gail cleared her throat pointedly. "We'll be grilling later when your dad gets home, if you want to stop over for dinner," she offered. My father wouldn't be home for at least another two hours. Maybe I'd have time to take that shower.

"Sure, maybe, thanks." Neither Stepmother Gail nor I were very good at casual conversation anymore. Well, at least not with each other. I loved my father, but Dad wasn't exactly the warm and fuzzy Ward Cleaver type, and he'd long ago tired of the drama, deciding to let Gail and I work out our relationship, or lack of one, for ourselves.

She gathered up her half-filled coffee cup, as well as Denise's, and moved toward the kitchen. I followed behind her slowly, carrying my own cup and handing it to her absently as she finished rinsing the other two, popping them all in the dishwasher, green on the left, blue on the right. Her glance fell on the disorganized coffee carousel, and I sensed more than saw her shoulders tighten. And then she sighed. She wasn't the least bit surprised. I guess maybe it said something about my behavior of late. I moved around her and began reorganizing the mess I'd made, keeping my back to her. Maybe it had been a childish and unnecessary thing to do, after all.

"Thanks," she breathed behind me. "I know it probably seems like a silly thing..."

I turned around, the counter against my back. She stood closer than I anticipated and regarded me cautiously. Her thoughtfulness regarding my mother's things was unexpected. Okay, maybe not so much unexpected on her part, as failure to recognize the overture on mine. It probably wasn't the first time.

Well, this was awkward.

"We all have our little quirks." I shrugged with a forced smile and took a deep breath. "You have a pathological need for order. Me? Well..." I laughed in an unwelcome moment of self-awareness. "Maybe we

16

shouldn't even open that overstuffed can of worms." I straightened and she quickly stepped back.

I took a deep breath. "About the furniture…I didn't realize…I mean, I always thought…" I began ineptly. The truth was, I always believed she'd disposed of any and every material thing hinting at my mother's existence and lamented I couldn't be discarded quite so easily. Gail waved me off and turned to pull on a knob. She began to nervously and unnecessarily organize the already perfectly perfect silverware drawer. "Well, anyway I just want to say thank you. I appreciate it."

She could have said a lot of things. She could have said I was an ungrateful brat. She could have said I never missed an opportunity to irritate or intimidate her. She could have said that in my eyes, she'd always been damned if she did and damned if she didn't. And she wouldn't have been far off the mark. But, she said none of those things. She simply nodded. Acknowledging my stepmother might actually be a person with a heart who could consequently be affected, nay, hurt, by my digs and indifference was a foreign concept to me. Probably because I'd always considered her an unwelcome interloper who distracted my father from more important things—namely me.

But, eighteen months ago, I had been at my lowest point, and I'd crawled back here like a wounded dog looking for…something. Comfort, maybe. Some reinforcement to confirm I was still someone worth loving despite that scene at Alberto's when I found Roger and Barbara sharing a booth and Alberto slapped me with a lifetime ban.

Well, sure, I know red wine stains, but how was I to know truffles were so expensive? Fungus is fungus to me. I do miss his Spaghetti alla Carbonara, though.

Dad had patted me on the back and told me things would get better. Gail didn't say much, probably suspecting, from past experience, that I wouldn't welcome her input. Instead, she'd tried to give me back a piece of my birth mother, tried to show me, without words, that how I felt mattered. And I hadn't even had the courtesy to notice. She never mentioned it, never tried to take credit for it, and if she was hurt I didn't acknowledge the gesture, she never showed it. I guess it did make her the bigger person. It was second nature to blame my antagonism toward Gail, on Gail.

Have I mentioned I don't do well with change?

"I'll see you later," I said as I opened the door. "I'll uh, bring a salad or something." It wasn't exactly an apology, or a promise of new beginnings, but I thought it was as good an exit line as any, and it was probably as civil as I'd been to my stepmother in a long time.

Chapter Two

Between the heat, the espresso, the unforeseen discovery of my stepmother's humanity, and doing double duty on the stairs, I was feeling a little shaky by the time I reached the sanctuary of my OBOG and took a deep whiff of the soothing cinnamon scent wafting from the air freshener disintegrating on the kitchen counter. Caesar had finished his tuna surprise while I was gone and settled himself in a shaft of late afternoon sunlight stretching warm, inviting fingers of golden heat across middle of the living room floor. I rinsed and dried his bowl and gave him some fresh water. He was snoring loudly, somewhere between a purr and a wheeze, flat on his back, four paws in the air, his enormous gray and white girth spread out, looking like Shamu's furry cousin. He didn't deign to acknowledge my return. He is, after all, a feline. Me? I'm merely the staff. There is nothing like a cat to make a girl sympathize with Rodney Dangerfield's characteristic lament for respect.

I kicked off my flip flops and grabbed the mail from the basket on the rickety table inside the door where I'd been letting it accumulate since Monday. I perched on one of the padded wrought iron barstools lined up on the living room side of the island and began listlessly sorting through it, separating the monthly bills from the junk mail and weekly flyers. I was beyond thrilled to discover I could name my price on car insurance, get an online degree in flower arranging, or, if I was feeling especially daring, pursue a rewarding career as a cosmetics representative. I tossed most of it in the trash, although the way my search for employment was progressing, the last one might have been a keeper. Then again, the search would probably be more productive if I actually went out and applied for something. I approached the job market the way some people approached the lottery. They dream of winning, but never buy a ticket.

I slid from the stool and looked around. The place looked no different than it had when I went next door, but I saw it now with new eyes. These were things my mother had chosen, things she'd loved. I was surrounded by a time when I still believed life was perfect, a time before mothers died, a time before abandonment issues, and adulterous husbands. I ran my hands along the sofa here, the back of a chair there, trying to re-capture some memory, some feeling of when that belief had been real. Why had I not noticed the furniture sooner? Probably because I was busy concentrating on the fact that everything was used, leftover, cast off, just like me. I thought Gail was trying to make a point. She was. I apparently missed it. Completely.

I still had a least an hour before my father, the Grill Master, would be home. Every spring, when the new models arrive at Logan's Hardware, as predictably as daylight savings time, Dad backs his beat up pickup into the drive and unloads the latest and greatest enamel coated steel atrocity of the season. I'd like to go on record as saying that as far as I am concerned, a grill is a grill is a grill. Light the fire, slap down the meat, flip and serve. Pretty basic stuff.

Not to Dad. The Hardware King of Hamilton is, in fact, a closet barbecue junkie. This year he's rocking a Char-Griller Duo S-5050 combination gas and charcoal number with 1260 square inches of cooking area and a stay cool handle, electric ignition, and removable grease catcher. A big, shiny black baby with a 12000 BTU cast brass side burner and cast iron grates. He claims he was drawn to the obvious advantage of having both gas and charcoal capability—the convenience of the gas, and deliciousness of the charcoal, with the possibility of learning to smoke meats as well. So far, he's used it a total of three times. But, he has every episode of Grillin' with Robbie Ray on DVR, so as soon as he can tear himself away from the store, he's all set. Dad is pretty much a workaholic, although I have occasionally noticed the bluish flicker of a lonely TV emanating from the windows of his home office in the wee hours when I walk the floor fighting my ongoing battle with insomnia.

I opened the fridge to see what I had in the way of salad fixings, since I'd so recklessly offered to provide one. I felt that in this new spirit of détente I should put a little more effort into it than my usual wilted lettuce in a bowl. I decided I could sacrifice my one remaining bag of mixed field greens, some organic grape tomatoes, crumbled feta, a handful of black olives, and some sliced red onion. My pantry cabinet coughed up some chopped walnuts and the remainder of a bag of dried cranberries. All in all, it looked pretty good and smelled even better, although I'd possibly been overly enthusiastic with the onions.

I wrestled with a sheet of plastic wrap, slicing the side of my thumb on the little metal saw thing that never actually works on the plastic wrap but always manages to slice through skin just fine. I eventually managed to stretch a piece over most of the top of the bowl, and popped it back in the fridge next to a bottle of fat free poppy seed dressing I didn't plan to add until the last minute so everything would stay nice and crisp. I detest soggy salad. I wondered if I should bring a bottle of wine. I felt around under the sink and came up with a dusty bottle of particularly nice Chianti I'd been saving for a special occasion. Special occasions have been few and far between lately, as you may have already guessed. Steak on the patio with Dad and Gail wasn't exactly cause for celebration. I mean, I didn't think Gail and I were on the verge of becoming best friends or anything. I was harboring no illusions we would sit around the Char-Griller Duo S-5050 later, hold hands, and sing Kumbaya. But, I guess it was significant that now I could *maybe* acknowledge she wasn't the root of all evil.

So okay, I should probably take the wine.

Sir Chicken Caesar still hadn't moved, nor did he so much as twitch when I tossed my damp T-shirt over him after peeling it off my sticky body on my way into the bathroom. He has his priorities—sleep being one, food the other. I fell somewhere near the bottom of his list, only slightly above hairballs.

I stripped down to my thirty-five-year-old birthday suit, avoiding my reflection in the full length mirror on the closet door, and yanked open the top dresser drawer to peruse the underwear selection and simply savor the delicious coolness of AC on damp, bare skin. Steak on the patio did not seem to demand sexy lingerie, then again, nothing in my life these days did, and serviceable cotton Grammy panties would be far more practical in the heat. I grabbed a pair from the top of the pile and added shorts and a fresh tank from one of the laundry baskets near the bathroom door. One for clean clothes, one for dirty. Guess which one had the bigger pile? The only household chore I love more than laundry is standing on a chair in the living room and letting the ceiling fan whack me in the head. Repeatedly.

At last I had everything I needed and stepped over the threshold and into my own personal Shangri-La. The bathroom was a masterpiece of black Italian marble, chrome, and glass. I reached into the shower and activated my absolute favorite thing in the entire apartment: my Chastings Corque Corian Square Ceiling Mount Showerhead. Okay, so my dad owns the hardware store and had gotten the fixture at a deep discount, but still, it felt like the ultimate in decadent luxury every time I stepped under the water. For ten to twenty minutes a day, I was Jane, naked in the rainforest, lulled by the mysterious sounds of the African jungle, sunlight dappling the forest floor, waiting under the waterfall for my Tarzan to swing down from the nearest Angouma tree. Hey, you have your fantasies and I have mine.

Perhaps the only drawback to the licentious luxury of Italian marble is the fact that when combined with soap, shampoo, and water, it has a tendency to become the slick equivalent of an Olympic ice skating rink. I know this because I am a reasonably intelligent woman. I actually earned a B+ in physics. I also know this because when I first moved in, I managed to land on my bare, wet ass on more than one occasion.

I just could not bring myself to deface my lovely white veined marble with those tacky stick-on vinyl fish in order to attain some semblance of traction and safety. I did, however, break down and buy a rubber bathmat that I could, and did, remove and hide under the bathroom sink after every use. Preoccupied as I was with the unexpected developments in my relationship with the she-devil next door, on this particular occasion, the mat slipped (no pun intended) my mind. In retrospect, it was probably a mistake.

The unthinkable happened right after soap and rinse, and right before repeat. As usual, I dropped my luxury cotton crocheted bath puff, heavy with water and oozing with soap foam. With my eyes closed against the burn of the shampoo running down my face, I felt around with my bare foot in an attempt to locate it. I clutched it between my bare toes and then tried a careful, if ungainly, squat to retrieve it. Like there was anyone there to see me? It was then I felt my feet go out from under me. But, instead of landing on my well-padded derriere, as I usually did, my head took the brunt of the impact, cracking against the beautiful, cool marble floor with a sickening thud. My last coherent thought before everything went black? "Shoot, that's gonna leave a mark."

****

I opened my eyes slowly, slightly surprised I could even see straight after the whack I'd taken. I gingerly crawled into a seated position, thinking my head should hurt far worse than it did. I immediately realized I was no longer in the shower. The most likely scenario seemed to be that I lay unconscious in an ambulance on the way to Beaumont South ER while enjoying a particularly vivid dream en route.

It certainly didn't occur to me that I was dead.

Not right away, at least. Why would it? Nothing I'd ever been taught in the Saint Sofia's Religious Education classes Gail insisted both Denise and I attend until age thirteen, long after our friends had gotten a reprieve, could have prepared me for an afterlife resembling an abandoned bus station looking like it had last been redecorated—and cleaned—circa nineteen seventy-three. The air reeked of burnt coffee, stale urine, and old disinfectant. The latter burned my nose and caused my eyes to water. Empty cups and old newspapers littered the floor, and an orderly row of orange plastic chairs sat chained together along the far wall adding a nice institutional touch and reminding me of the Office of Public Welfare downtown. I wondered if the chains were strictly necessary. I mean, who would want to steal them?

Contrary to popular belief, I saw no ethereal, pearly gate, but there were two enormous doors made of what looked like stainless steel glinting beneath garish, neon signs worthy of the Vegas strip. Over one, a flashing blue arrow pointed north, and over the other, a blinking red one pointed south. The message on the arrows was written in some symbolic hieroglyphic language defying translation, but honestly, it didn't take a rocket scientist to figure it out. I guess even the afterlife was striving for political correctness and cultural sensitivity these days. No matter what your country of origin, religious beliefs, or native tongue, even an illiterate, heathen, cave-dwelling headhunter knows the difference between up and down. That's when I began to worry.

There were no celestial choirs, no clouds, and not a single angel in sight. But, I slowly became aware of a strange looking little man hunched over the gray metal desk that occupied the space between the gates—er, elevators. Small and wiry, in an ill-fitting brown flannel suit, he looked grim and harried, tapping away on a computer keyboard, his frown deepening with every stroke. His eyes were glued to the screen and his head was bent to look over, instead of through, his gold wire bifocals.

Poor guy, I had the same problem with mine no matter what prescription they gave me. It was so frustrating.

Light from some unseen overhead source reflected on the bits of his bald scalp peeking out boldly between the strands of his oh-so-sexy comb-over. He paid no attention to me whatsoever, further bolstering my hope that this might be nothing more than a bad dream. My head still throbbed where it had made contact with the marble, and I knew I'd definitely cracked my skull hard enough to scramble my brain into a realistic three dimensional hallucination such as this. Quite possibly I had a concussion. Maybe even a subdural hematoma. Perhaps I would need a craniotomy. I hoped Brad-the-Famous-Vascular-Surgeon could recommend a good neurologist.

There didn't seem to be anyone else around, so I carefully picked my way across the newspaper-littered floor to the room's only other occupant.

"Excuse me," I said politely. Given the average number of deaths per day in the United States alone is over six-thousand, it seemed unlikely I would be the solitary occupant of the "waiting room," or whatever they called this place, if I'd actually died. I looked around hopefully. Yep, I was still the only one here.

"Take a number," he mumbled in an irritated voice without looking up.

"You've got to be kidding."

"Protocol," he intoned distantly. "Take a number and have a seat." He glanced over the top of his wire rimmed bifocals and did a quick head to toe. He swallowed hard and shifted uncomfortably before reaching under the desk and pulling out a clumsily folded towel. "And cover up, if it wouldn't be too much trouble."

I glanced down and realized that everything I owned was on display. Well, I had been taking a shower, after all. I certainly would have dressed for the occasion had I known. It did put all of those dreams of showing up at high school assembly in my underwear into perspective, though. Arriving naked for an appointment with eternity was infinitely more humiliating. I hurriedly grabbed the proffered towel and wrapped it around my assets, tucking the end securely into my cleavage. I plucked a plastic card from the top of the pile, hoping the system here was more expedient than the SuperSave deli. Forty-five minutes for a half a pound of Genoa salami is definitely what anyone would consider an unacceptable wait time. Then I stomped over to claim a manacled seat. I had my choice, so I played eenie, meenie, minie, moe and ended up with the one in the center. I had no sooner settled myself, and realized my backside immediately stuck to something on the seat—what I did *not* want to know—when Bifocal Boy seemed to finish working on whatever had his features twisted into knots.

"Next," he intoned solemnly, looking straight at me.

I made quite a show of looking around, as though unsure to whom he was referring. I raised an eyebrow and pointed to myself in surprise, whereupon he rolled his eyes and waved me forward with a tight-lipped frown. I made my way back to the desk, kicking aside a few discarded fast food restaurant cups with the reference to John 3:16 printed under the rim, and plunked the plastic card back on the pile with a decisive click. He waved me into an upholstered chair that hadn't been there before, and was not chained to anything else. It was only slightly more comfortable than the sticky plastic seat had been. Apparently they weren't looking for anyone to become too attached to the place. No problem here. I was ready and willing, if apparently unable, to return to my own wet and soapy shower stall anytime. The sooner, the better, actually.

"Name?" His fingers were once again poised over his keyboard.

"Shouldn't you already know that?" I retorted smartly, feeling better by the minute. After all, if I was really dead, surely someone would have been expecting me. In fact, I think my grandma would probably have been there to meet me, maybe with cookies or something. At least, that's what all of the near death experience survivors say.

See, I did pay attention in Sunday school. Well, at least until about age ten after which time I hid the latest horror novel inside my Catechism. Sister Mary Eloise, better known among the Sunday school set as Sister Myrtle Elephant, never suspected a thing. Of course, she was almost ninety, legally blind, and more than slightly hard of hearing, so I guess pulling one over on her was probably no great accomplishment on my part.

"Protocol," he repeated wearily.

"Naturally," I returned sarcastically. "Maxine Esmeralda Logan McCoy."

"Esmeralda?" He smirked.

"Family name... Can we get on with this? I have somewhere to be when I wake up."

"Oh, my dear." He chuckled heartily as his fingers clacked over the keys. "If I had a nickel for every time I've heard that one I could...well, I'd have an awful lot of nickels!" He peered at the screen and began to frown again. He typed in a few more commands, hit enter, and sat back with a grunt, his face paling before my eyes.

"You aren't in here."

"Of course I'm not in there." It was my turn to smirk. "This is a dream. Not a particularly *sanitary* dream," I muttered as I lifted my feet one at a time to wipe them with the end of the towel, "but a dream all the same. I imagined Heaven would be a little cleaner."

"This isn't Heaven," he replied crossly, "it's the Office of Central Processing, better known as the OCP. And I'm sorry to disappoint you, but this is definitely not a dream. You are unquestionably dead, but something isn't right. Your name is not in my database."

He seemed pretty certain of my demise and a tight knot of fear began to form beneath the damp towel draped around my chest. Experts agree the bathroom is the second most dangerous room in the house. Hard to believe, but one person dies everyday while using the bathtub in the United States. Three hundred and forty-five people of all ages died in bathtubs in nineteen eighty-nine alone. Honest. You can Google it. But I hadn't been in a bathtub. I'd been in an elegantly appointed Italian Marble shower. Death should be forbidden to touch someone surrounded by Italian marble enjoying the trickling pseudo rainfall of a Chastings Corque Corian Square Ceiling Mount Showerhead. I was going to thank Gail for that, too, when I got back, I swear.

I could not be dead. I was only thirty-five years old and in excellent health, for a dead chick. I still had things to do, places to go, people to see. And I planned to, just as soon as I got the motivation to leave my apartment. I closed my eyes and clicked my heels three times. I wiggled my nose. I wished on a falling star. If Marvin wasn't hogging the keyboard, I would have hit Ctrl+Alt+Del. I took a deep breath and opened my eyes. Nothing had changed.

"That's impossible," I said in a flat voice that sounded far calmer than you would expect under the circumstances. "I'm not in your database. Obviously there's been a mistake. Just send me back, and we'll call it even. It'll be our little secret."

Elizabeth Kubler-Ross documented five stages of grieving. Other authorities have identified up to seven. But, no matter which theory you subscribe to, all have one thing in common: the first stage is denial. I planned to keep my butt firmly planted in stage one, *Denial* with a capital D.

Marvin Jenks, so said his little brass nameplate, was huddled over the keyboard, typing furiously, mumbling something about SSIs on maternity leave, incompetent trainees, and an inept IT department. Over his grousing, I heard footsteps behind me and turned.

"*Buddy*?" I gasped. "What are *you* doing here?" The pimply cashier from the SuperSave offered me an apologetic purple grin and shifted uncomfortably from one foot to the other.

"Hey," he raised a limp hand in greeting, looking past me nervously toward old Marv who was glaring at him across the desk, his foot tapping out an angry, impatient staccato. "How's it going?

"How's it *going*? Well, apparently I'm *dead*, Buddy. I'm *dead* and eternity is an unkempt bus terminal. I'm *dead* and I'm not in the database, so apparently I can't even *die* right. Bottom line? I'm *dead*, Buddy! Everything is just wucking fonderful, thanks so much for asking."

Hmmm…seems despite my best intentions I had moved beyond Denial with a capital D and right on to Anger with a great big capital A.

Buddy was more than a little taken aback by my vehement response and seemed to shrink into himself before my eyes. I have no doubt he was enormously sorry he'd asked. Well, you know what they say about asking a stupid question.

"Language, Ms. Logan," Marvin admonished primly.

Seriously? He turned his attention to the visibly distraught cashier whose whole demeanor was beginning to annoy me. Shouldn't I have the monopoly on distraught here?

"Well, GRIT 125, what do you have to say for yourself?" Marvin demanded tightly.

Buddy, aka GRIT 125, was twisting the hem of his red polyester vest into nervous knots.

"GRIT?"

"Grim Reaper in Training," Marvin replied absently. "Well?"

"Oops?" He tried the purple brace enhanced smile on Marvin with even less success than he'd had with me.

"Oops? That's your excuse for this mess? OOPS?" Marvin's face had gone from pale gray to mottled purple in less than a heartbeat. "You are *NOT* a Grim Reaper yet, young man, nor at this rate are you ever likely to be. You are a trainee...a *trainee*. You do *NOT* sever a soul from a body unless they are specifically referred to you by the SSI or under the *direct supervision* of a qualified, licensed and bonded Grim Reaper. Your actions today are in direct violation of everything in the training manual! Dammit, Buddy, it's the third time this month!"

His voice rose in volume about every third word, and by the end of his tirade I was forced to cover my ears or risk nerve deafness. Buddy was hanging his head in shame, his expression hidden by a lank forelock of highlighted hair showing at least an inch of regrowth at the roots. Apparently hair care in the afterlife left something to be desired, too.

"Language, Mr. Jenks." I couldn't resist.

"The SSI is on maternity leave, and the Grim said he had someone for me," the cashier formerly known as Buddy replied defensively. "He said he'd get back to me with the particulars, but then when she came through my line today with her aura in tatters, I figured she must be the one and I'd make a good impression by getting the job done ahead of time."

My aura was in tatters? Huh. Guess that explains

why my mood ring stopped working.

"But she still *had* an aura, you idiot, which *should* have been your first clue. Now I have another D.I.E. on my hands, thanks to your incompetence. What do you suggest we do about it?"

"D.I.E.?" I interjected. Wow, they really love their acronyms here.

"Death in Error. It is not looked upon favorably by…" he rolled his eyes in the direction of the 'up' arrow. "Although, he," he rolled his eyes in the other direction, "is not so particular."

I agreed with the up guy. I didn't look upon it very favorably myself at the moment. "Well, in that case," I replied in relief, "just send me back. Seriously. No hard feelings. These things happen. Kids, huh? I completely understand. I won't mention a thing to your boss. I promise. I won't even call my lawyer. I'll sign a waiver. You will never hear from me again."

"I'm afraid it isn't quite that simple," Marv began.

"What about me?" GRIT 125 interrupted with a whine. "Will this go on my permanent record? It was an accident…" Marvin looked as annoyed as I felt at the interruption, and I'd had about all I could take from the little weasel. First he calls me ma'am, and then he kills me to impress his boss. He really was on my last nerve.

"Listen carefully, Buddy. I. Am. Dead. But wait…let's forget about me for a minute, and the fact my being here in the first place is *all your fault.* Let's pay attention to *you* and all of *your* needs," I ground out between my teeth.

He stifled the whining. He also took a great big step back. Maybe he wasn't quite as dumb as he looked, after all.

33

I turned back to my new pal, Marvin. "Ok, Marv…how do we fix this?"

Marvin spread his hands helplessly, and shook his head.

I cut him off before he could open his mouth. "Don't say it, Marv. Do *not* say we can't fix this. I am totally not prepared to die today. I didn't cancel my cable. I didn't lock the door. I'm pretty sure I left the stove on." Okay, so I don't cook, but Marv didn't know that. At least I didn't think he did. "I forgot to let the cat out. Do you have any idea what kind of mess that can lead to?" Marvin's expression didn't change. He wasn't buying it, and my panic escalated. "Hey, I know! That little plastic number said I was customer one thousand. I bet there's some kind of second chance bonus prize for the thousandth customer, right?"

I could not be dead, totally and irrevocably dead. My life wasn't perfect, but hope springs eternal. I was still busy figuring it out. Look at today, for instance. Gail and I had almost had an actual conversation. That must count for something. Sure there'd been days when I'd been despondent enough to wonder if I might be better off dead, but not like this. Not…death by soap. Was there supposed to be a moral in there somewhere? If so, it escaped me completely.

I felt a little bubble of hysteria struggling to the surface. I forced it down. This wasn't fate. I wasn't meant to die today. I knew it. My name did not appear in the database. There was a way to fix this. There had to be a way to fix this. Bargaining! The next step in the Kubler-Ross model was bargaining. Everybody has an angle. I simply had to figure out Marvin's and determine how I could work it to my advantage.

"What's an SSI?" I asked with a sudden flash of brilliance.

"Huh?" Marv appeared visibly confused by the sudden change in topic.

"An SSI...what is it?"

"You have no need to know that."

"Humor me, Marv."

"Why?"

"Well, if I understand correctly, this SSI person is on maternity leave. Looks like you are a man down, or should I say woman down, given the whole maternity thing? I'm going to go out on a limb and assume this SSI has nothing to do with the federal income supplement program of the same name funded by general tax revenues."

"Oh." Marvin blinked behind his bifocals like an owl caught in headlights. "No...no, of course it doesn't. An SSI is a Superintendent of Spiritual Impediment. It's a regional position. Some souls, though not all, have unfinished business at the time of death." He nodded toward me with a tight smile. "I'm sure you can relate, what with your cable, stove, and cat issues. Anyway, the SSI is a go-between, a kind of social worker who attempts to rectify any issue or concern, i.e. unfinished business, which hinders said spirit from advancing to the next phase of existence. Once all problems have been addressed as best they can be, the Grim Reaper severs the soul from the mortal plane and the spirit is able to move on." His brows lowered again as he spared another glare for the whimpering Buddy who had gone scythe happy and caused this whole mess. "It's a very efficient process, usually."

I leaned back in my chair and adjusted the towel

around me carefully as I crossed and re-crossed my legs a la Sharon Stone. "I assume your butt is going to be in a sling over this?" Butter wouldn't melt in my mouth, but the daggers shooting from old Marv's eyes when he glanced at Buddy surely would have sliced and diced it.

"Not exactly, but I expect I'll be hearing about it." Sweat poured off of the little guy in amounts copious enough to overpower even the scent of the disinfectant. He was lying. For some reason, his ass was totally grass over this.

This whole fiasco had become exhausting—whacking my head, waking up dead, maintaining my Denial with a capital D, tamping down my Anger with a capital A, and trying to formulate a Bargain with a capital B, that had slightly more than a snowball's chance in hell of getting me out of here. If the current SSI was on maternity leave, logically she must be a living breathing person. I needed to return to my life as a living breathing person. Marv needed an SSI. I needed a job. Granted, if I ever thought for a New York minute any potential job might entail my becoming a counselor to the generally reluctant to be deceased, I would at least have taken some continuing education classes or something. Of course, it could be worse. I could have gotten a call back for the position of cashier at the SuperSave. Red polyester and I are not friends.

"Well, Marv, I'd like to make you an OYCR." It was a testament to my desperation that up until this afternoon I didn't even believe in ghosts. Well, except the ones on Ghost Encounters. I mean, who wouldn't believe *those* guys? Now I was about to volunteer to be the champion of the corporeally challenged. At least temporarily, assuming I truly was dead and this wasn't some bizarre dream brought about by an unhealthy dependence on Chinese take-out. Yes, I still waffled between Denial and Anger, but anything that got my towel-wrapped soul reunited with the cold, wet butt back in my shower was okay by me. Marvin pulled a snowy square of linen from inside his jacket and mopped at his dripping brow.

"OYCR?"

"Offer You Can't Refuse. Acronyms seem to be awfully popular around here. A girl likes to fit in. What's wrong? Don't you have that one in your little office manual, Marv?"

"Oh, I see, you're making a joke, right? Ha." He didn't appear amused. "For your information, Ms. Logan, the OCP is mired in bureaucratic paperwork. We find acronyms quite useful. Big timesavers, you know."

"I can only imagine," I responded dryly.

"Now, what did you have in mind?" The fact he was even willing to hear me out and possibly negotiate told me he was in far more trouble than he let on. My girl power meter began to quiver and rise to attention.

"I need my life back, and I coincidentally need a job. You have an unregistered erroneously acquired soul, aka D.I.E. you don't know what to do with *and* you need a Superintendent of Spiritual Impediment." He opened and closed his mouth several times, like a gasping fish. You know how they look when you take them off the hook and they lie there on the dock wondering where the hell the water went? Yep, exactly like that. "I don't belong here, Marv. I know it, you know it. You owe me, Marv. Bottom line? You send me back and no one is the wiser. Plus, you get yourself a temporary SSI."

I had one more condition. Okay, maybe I was pushing my luck, but nothing ventured, nothing gained, right? "And Buddy the Bungler here gets put on suspension until the real SSI is back from maternity leave." I might not be in any position to dictate, but I like to rely on the power of positive thinking.

Right.

"Uncle Marvin, not suspension, *please...*" wailed Buddy in an even whinier voice.

Uncle Marvin? Well, that explained a lot. And didn't Marvin say this had been The Budster's third snafu this month? Ah, things were looking up. My heart kicked me in the ribs and began to beat. I swallowed over a painful lump in my throat when I realized it hadn't been beating at all before now. Marvin glowered Buddy into silence and reached into the top drawer of his desk, slapping a small, brown, leather bound book on the desk between us.

"This is most irregular, but if I have to account for one more D.I.E. this month...well, let's just say there's a reason they say you shouldn't hire relatives. Review this book prior to performing any spiritual interventions. You'll find everything you need in Appendix A. Memorize it and sign the waiver on page one before you start. Please remember this is a temporary position. Actually, it shouldn't be for much longer, but the other SSIs have been covering and I'm sure they'll appreciate the help. Someone will contact you when Alicia, the SSI for the Northeast Region, is fit to resume her duties. At that time, all powers and privileges of the office of SSI will cease. You hold up your end of the bargain, and your life is yours." He stood and offered his hand. "You have a deal, Ms. Logan. Don't make me regret it."

"I get powers and privileges? You mean like superpowers? Cool beans! Can I fly now or anything? Kinda sucks that you giveth and then you taketh away, but, hey, all things considered, I can live with it." Because the important thing was that I would *live*. "Hey Marv, what happened to the other D.I.E.s?"

"Why, they stayed dead, of course," he said, as though it should have been obvious.

"But, why? That doesn't seem fair."

"Few things are, my dear. They never considered there was any other option." He withdrew his hand with a conspiratorial wink. "I guess they never read Kubler-Ross."

I stood too, clutching my towel with one hand, and just that quickly he was gone. Along with the towel. I felt the cold caress of black Italian marble against my bare butt. I gasped for air while coughing and choking on the snootful of water pouring up my nose from the Chastings Corque Corian Square Ceiling Mount Showerhead above me. My head screamed with the agony of a thousand jackhammers, and over the scent of my Sensual Amber body wash, I perceived the sweet, copper tang of blood. Excruciating pain had never felt so good. Hallelujah, I was back! But, I was definitely going to need stitches.

Chapter Three

The initial euphoria I felt at finding myself naked, wet, and bleeding on the floor of my dangerously slick Italian marble shower soon gave way to the realization I was in a rather bad state. I reached to the back of my head and then squinted at my hand, which seemed to be covered in an inordinately large amount of blood. I also absently noted the water swirling into the drain looked more crimson than clear. Everyone knows that anatomically, the skin on the head is a little on the thin side, and physiologically, the blood pressure in the head is slightly higher than it is elsewhere in the body. It therefore seems reasonable to assume a whole lot of blood can force its way out of a comparatively small wound.

Everyone also knows the reason so much blood is sent to the head is because the human brain needs so much energy. Judging by the volume I was losing, compounded by the rate of the flow, I had either sustained more than a small wound or my brain was the size of the Chicago Bean. Despite this obvious irrefutable physical proof I must be incredibly bright, I had to admit I felt a little faint. Okay, maybe more than a little. I figured that trying to stand up in the soap-and-blood-slicked shower might not be the best way to exhibit my supposed superior intelligence. So I crawled out, stiffly and carefully, and made slow and painful progress across the floor. I crawled up the toilet and groped at the vanity until I achieved relative verticality.

I blindly grabbed the first towel that came to hand and clapped it to my head, wincing at the resultant painful burn. I winced again—this time in dismay—when I realized I'd grabbed one of the Carrere Luxor Bath Towels Denise had given me last Christmas. She'd custom ordered them from Italy six weeks ahead of time. While I would never indulge in such extravagance myself, I had to admit, something about wrapping up in seven hundred gram, 100% cotton terry after a shower soothed the soul. The towel was white, of course. I wondered if Santa would bring me a replacement. Or a very large bottle of bleach.

Somehow I managed to stay on my feet, holding on to the counter and closing my eyes until the room stopped spinning, and then attempted an awkward one handed swipe maneuver with another towel until I was able to dry most of my body. I still felt damp and sticky—and not in a good way—but it was the best I could do. I donned my cotton undies and cargo shorts, still limited to one hand and a number of contortions I hadn't known I could perform. The dexterity required for donning a bra was beyond me, so I allowed the girls to roam free while I squirmed into my tank and struggled to keep the ruined towel plastered to my scalp. I heard my cell ringing in the bedroom, and even that distant jangle made me see stars. I sighted down the bathroom and took aim at the doorway. A straight line may be the shortest distance between two points, but my brain hadn't sent my feet the memo, and my progress would have done me proud on a bunny slope slalom course.

The phone stopped ringing by the time I reached it. Naturally. The screen showed a missed call from Gail at six-eighteen. My stomach, which already felt queasy—what with falling, dying, being sent back, and finding myself in the throes of a massive hemorrhage, all in the space of an afternoon—began to churn in earnest. I calculated I must have been out for over an hour. That was probably a bad thing, right? Even more unsettling was the site of Marv's little brown book on the bed next to the phone. Either I hadn't been dreaming, or I still was. Both scenarios were equally disturbing. Gail had left a voice message to tell me the steaks were done. I hit redial.

Sorry to ruin your dinner folks, but I think I need a doctor.

Gail took one look at me and insisted on calling an ambulance. There is nothing I love more than being the neighborhood curiosity. Everyone on the street turned out to watch the emergency responders carry me out of my apartment and load me into the ambulance. They stood around the end of the drive rubbernecking until it zipped away with sirens blaring, while Gail and Dad followed in her car. One benefit of using the local paramedic as your chauffeur is you don't spend any time at all in the waiting room. Nope. My blood-gushing head and I were taken into a trauma bay stat. An overzealous nurse who had obviously seen way too many television medical dramas managed to shred most of my clothes with her trusty bandage scissors before I managed to convince her my only injury was the one on my head. Fortunately, I wasn't wearing a hat, it would have been toast. So here I was, thirteen stainless steel staples, one CT scan, and a probable concussion later, fashionably garbed in a hospital gown with busted ties, courtesy of the previously referenced maniacal television fan, with my ass flapping in the wind.

I was currently arguing with a reasonably attractive twenty-something ER resident who was insisting I spend the night. Oh, not with him. In the observation ward. Had he suggested the former, I might have been tempted to give it more serious consideration. The strong tone of condescension lacing his voice made me grit my teeth.

Okay, so maybe that hurt me far more than it did him.

"Look, I get it. But, trust me when I tell you that you cannot imagine the day I've had. I just want to go home. My folks will be here with my clothes any minute. If my headache gets worse, if my vision changes, if I get confused, start vomiting, find myself talking like the town drunk on Friday night, or see little twinkling stars spinning around my noggin like a Saturday morning cartoon…you will be the first to know, okay?" I thought maybe batting my eyelashes coyly to take the edge off of my sharp retort couldn't hurt.

Hmm…surprise, I found out it could.

At that point, I elected to close my eyes altogether until the throbbing subsided to a manageable level. This, of course, caused me to sway on my feet, which really didn't bolster my argument for discharge.

"Look, Ms. Logan," he said, grabbing my arm to hold me steady. "You seem to know what you're talking about, but my recommendation is that you be admitted for observation." He drew his brows together in his most intimidating "I am physician, hear me roar" expression.

Yeah, that doesn't really work on me. Unfortunately for him and his unibrow, I had experience with many physicians, and extensive experience with one physician in particular. Bottom line? They scratch their crotch in the morning, clip their toenails over the sink, and fart all night when they go out for Mexican food, just like everyone else.

Not quite so intimidating when you think about them like that, is it?

"If you insist on leaving, I'd suggest someone stay with you, at least for the next twenty-four hours or so." Well, Dad didn't do sickbed duty and would be next to useless. And he also had a tendency to talk loud— really, really loud. Shout, actually. Gail usually lapsed into an anaphylactic stupor if she got within twenty feet of Caesar. I'd never get any rest at all with all of that snorting, honking, and wheezing going on. Nope, I'd just sleep in my own little bed and set the alarm. After all, I'd already died once today. What were the chances of a repeat performance?

"Are you going to discharge me before sunrise, or do I have to sign out Against Medical Advice?"

I heard the door open and felt a cool breeze caress my bare buttocks. Before I had a chance to fully enjoy it, I realized there was a good chance of flashing the entire hallway. I reached around and tugged the ends of the figure flattering garment closed in a futile attempt to salvage some small measure of dignity. It was too late. I had been recognized.

"Max?" came the astonished voice of the one man on the planet who could be counted on to recognize a person by nothing more than a quick glimpse of ass:

Roger-the-Proctologist. He came around to stand beside Unibrow the Boy Wonder, who was still gripping my arm. That and sheer determination spared me the embarrassment of an undignified face plant on the green linoleum floor. Would this day never end? "Karen saw them bringing you in. What in the hell happened? Why didn't you call me?"

"For God's sake, Roger. Why would I call you?" Ouch, ouch, ouch. Indoor voice, Max, indoor voice.

"Because I'm your...because I'm a doctor," he finished self-consciously.

"Well, if I fall and break my ass, Roger, you'll be the first one on my list, m'kay?" I peeled the Boy Wonder's fingers away from my upper arm and shuffled to the bed, still clutching the gown across my backside. I climbed in, careful to reveal nothing, and pulled the sheet up to my chin.

"How's Bombshell?" I asked, proud of how supremely disinterested I sounded.

"It's Barbara," he corrected tightly, though we both knew the error had been deliberate. "And she's in South Beach at the moment." He turned to Boy Wonder. "Dr. Craig, I'm sure you have other business to attend to?"

"Actually, Dr. McCoy, I was trying to persuade Ms. Logan it is a very bad idea for her to go home alone. Maybe you'll have better luck. She's had quite a blow to the head and..."

"HIPAA, HIPAA, HIPAA," I admonished. "I haven't signed a single thing giving you permission to share my confidential medical information with this man. Therefore, I invoke my rights as described in the Health Insurance Portability and Accountability Act of Nineteen ninety-six. I'm sure you're familiar with it.

One more word and I will own you, fella."

Judging by the heightened color in Boy Wonder's face, I suspected he might have a little problem with outspoken women. Or noncompliant patients. Or perhaps he suffered from hypertension. I felt a twinge of concern. Or a pang of indigestion. Sometimes it's difficult to differentiate. Before I could open my mouth to suggest that he have one of the nurses check his blood pressure, he closed my chart with an angry snap and strode stiffly from the room. Touchy little resident. I was glad hospital doors are designed not to slam since the local anesthetic was starting to wear off and the jackhammer operator in my head had just returned from his lunch break.

"So, South Beach. I heard there's some wicked undertow down there this week. Luckily, she has those built in flotation devices. No chance of drowning there! No, Sir! Little Boobie…wait, scratch that…*Big* Boobie should be just fine."

"Are we really going to do this, Max?" he asked in a weary voice. "I came because I was worried about you. Just because we aren't married anymore doesn't mean I don't care about you." He liked using that line. A lot. In fact, if I had a nickel for every time he'd said it, well, as Marv observed, I'd have a lot of nickels. He came to stand beside the bed and reached for my hand. I didn't pull away, but I didn't squeeze back either. "You must be feeling like absolute crap. Do you still have to go for the jugular every time?"

"I don't know, Roger. It feels like I do." Because every time I saw him, it felt like something vital had been torn out of me all over again. Whoever said it was better to have loved and lost than to have never loved at all, obviously never had their heart ripped out of their chest. It hurt. It wasn't as if I loved him anymore. Okay, scratch that. I did love him. A part of me would always love him. I simply wasn't *in love* with him anymore. At least I didn't think I was. And didn't I have the right to hurt him for hurting me? I'm pretty sure I read that in Modern Divorcee. Or Divorce Digest. Or maybe it was TV Guide. Maybe giving up that right indicated a kind of forgiveness? I was pretty sure I wasn't ready to forgive him, but I also had enough functioning brain cells left to know this was probably not the ideal time to contemplate it one way or the other.

"You do know you should stay here tonight, right?"

"Yeah, and you do know you're wasting your breath, right?"

"What do you think?" His smile was sad as he squeezed my hand before pulling his away and tucking it in the pocket of his lab coat. "Well, your father sure isn't the type to play nursemaid and Gail is allergic to the cat. As I recall, it was one of the main reasons you wanted one. And Denise has the kids to worry about. So, if you aren't going to stay here, and I'm equally sure you won't stay at your father's, I guess I'll have to give you a call and check in every hour or so since you're too stubborn to do what you're told."

"Roger, it's been a really lousy day. I'm ready and willing for the Sleep Police to cuff me and take me away. The last thing I need to do is spend the night trading insults with you."

"I'm going to wake you up and make sure you haven't lapsed into a coma, not carry on a conversation.

47

Can't you just once take something I say at face value?"

"Been there, done that, Roger. See how well it worked out for me?" My eyes were closed against the glare of the overhead light, so I felt rather than saw him stiffen. "I'm tired, Roger. Isn't there an asshole in distress somewhere that's calling your name?"

"Well, I see your bitch switch is still working just fine, Max," he grumbled irritably. "Maybe one of these days you'll look in the mirror before you try and point out everything about me that didn't live up to your expectations."

I didn't bother to open my eyes. Sure, I was being a bitch, but it was the only way I knew how to interact with Roger anymore. Your husband cheats on you and then he wants to stay friends. Kind of feels like having your dog die and your mother telling you, you can still keep it. It really isn't the same.

"I'm sorry if you don't like my honesty, Roger, but to be fair, I didn't like your lies. Maybe you should think about how you treated me before you complain about how I react to it."

"Maybe you should do the same, Max."

I opened one eye and focused with difficulty on his flushed face. I hoped there would come a day when I could talk to him without being rude, sarcastic, or just plain mean, but today was not that day. Today had definitely been stronger than me, and it had totally kicked my butt. I'd already been physically and mentally exhausted before Roger showed up and added emotionally defeated to the mix.

"Is that the best you've got, Rog? What's next? You throw a Fruit Loop at me and expect it to hurt?" I didn't doubt Roger had an equally witty comeback, something like "neener, neener, neener", but fortunately Dad and Gail chose that moment to push through the door.

"Roger?" Both Dad and Gail looked slightly nonplussed.

Roger stepped away from the bed and headed for the door. "Dan, Gail." He nodded to them both and then called back as the door hissed shut. "Keep the phone by the bed, Max."

"What was he doing here?" Dad inquired as Gail began pulling my clothes from the bulky SuperSave bag.

I inched carefully out from between the institutionally starched sheets, thinking how remiss I had been in failing to appreciate my fifteen-hundred count Egyptian cotton sheets until now, and vowing to make it up to them by spending hours wrapped in their comfortable embrace as soon as I got home.

"He was doing what he does best, making a bad situation worse by aggravating the hell out of me." I grabbed the clothes and tugged the curtain around me while I struggled into them. I knew Gail had been the one to retrieve them from my laundry basket. One, because they actually matched, and two, because her eyes were as red and puffy as ripe plums indicating she and Caesar had been up close and personal. As long as I was decently covered and could go home, I wouldn't have cared if I was dressed like a clown, but it was nice of her to take one for the team.

"Um, hey thanks for bringing my things, Gail. I hope you took your antihistamines before you and Caesar spent any quality time together."

Stepmother Gail acknowledged my gratitude with a

series of uncontrolled sneezes on the other side of the curtain. Apparently, she'd forgotten the golden rule of prophylaxis in all of the excitement.

Three prescriptions, a tetanus shot, eight signatures, and a yellow carbon copy of my discharge instructions later, I was finally home. Gail had offered to stay, but frankly, being in the same room with Caesar caused her to be in more misery than I. I let her set the alarm clock, the oven timer, and the automatic 'on' for the television, and sent her home to her husband, her antihistamines, and her nasal spray. After she left, I went around and turned everything off again. I knew Roger would be calling every hour as threatened, no matter how unreceptive I'd been to the idea. He's tenacious like that. Also, he knows I hate to be disturbed when I'm sleeping, so he was probably tempted by the added perk of pissing me off.

My bed had been turned down, by Gail, no doubt, and when I changed into an oversized T-shirt and padded into the bathroom to brush my teeth, I saw the shower and bathroom had already been scrubbed clean. I knew Gail had done that, too. The place looked so clean and normal that if my head wasn't banging out a John Philip Sousa march, I could almost believe nothing out of the ordinary had happened. Well, my head banging and the little brown book on my nightstand under the phone, that is. I hadn't even had a chance to look at it yet, and it was not going to happen tonight, either. Gail had really come through for me today, or maybe I was only feeling shaky and miserable enough to appreciate it for a change.

I grabbed two ibuprophen from the medicine cabinet and washed them down with a gulp of water. I wasn't holding out much hope they would do more than maybe take the edge off, but not surprisingly, doctors weren't really keen on prescribing narcotic pain relief for head injuries, so my choices were limited. The antibiotic Doc Unibrow had prescribed required the rest of the glass. The thing was the size of a small country. I experimentally pushed my midsection against the bathroom counter to ensure I would be able to self-Heimlich should the need arise. Caesar had already made himself comfortable on the side of the bed that used to be Roger's, so I crawled into mine and closed my eyes with a contented sigh. It seemed like I had been sleeping for only a minute or two when my cell phone vibrated, jarring me from oblivion. I checked the screen, and as expected, it was Roger.

"Roger."

"Max. How are—"

I disconnected. Hey, I did warn him there would be no conversation. I dropped the phone back onto the nightstand with a satisfied smirk and rolled over.

Then I jerked upright and screamed loud enough to wake the dead, which had included me such a short time ago. It was enough to start up the conga line at the party inside my head all over again. Caesar had shifted his bulk to the foot of the bed, and in his place, staring at the ceiling was Old Man Taber. He was wearing his usual attire, a plaid flannel shirt, faded overalls, and steel toed work boots. His eyes were the washed out blue of a late winter sky, and he had wisps of white hair, sparse on his head, but thick on his face. He reminded me of a cachectic, lumberjack Santa and I was relatively sure he was dead. As a doornail.

Old Jeb had wandered off from the Shady Waste

Home for the Over the Hill and Terminally Inconvenient at the end of November.

Okay, so maybe it was actually called the Shady Rest Rehabilitation and Retirement Villa, but I think you get my point.

Hamilton isn't known for its mild winters, and then, of course, there's the river. All things considered, it would have been nothing short of a miracle if Jeb Taber hadn't perished within the first day or so of his disappearance.

"Max." He nodded pleasantly, turning his head slightly to face me as I cautiously slid out of the bed and perched in a chair across the room. I was careful not to make any sudden moves. I didn't want to startle him and have him start flying around the room or something. He looked much better than when I'd last seen him alive, younger, less care worn, more relaxed. Maybe it was the relief of casting off the old mortal coil or something.

"Mr. Taber," I acknowledged in a squeaky voice. "Um...how are you?"

"Well, obviously I'm dead... Still, I can't complain." He smiled, pale eyes twinkling. "How about yourself, Max?"

"Well, it's been kind of an interesting day, actually." I wondered if a neon sign flashing "Queen of Understatement" had appeared over my head. As soon as I could figure out how—hopefully there was something in the little brown book that would give me a clue—I was going to contact Marvin and give him a piece of my mind—assuming I had one left by morning. All things considered, he could have given me at least a twenty-four hour window to assume my new duties, whatever they entailed. And would it really have been too much trouble to send me back with my head in one piece considering my death had been his incompetent nephew's fault in the first place?

"Yeah, I heard something about that." Jeb chuckled, sitting up and dangling his feet over the end of the bed. "Being dead must have been quite a shock for you."

Yeah, it sure was. In the greater scheme of things, waking up to the ghost of the old man, who ran the corner store when I was a kid, lying in the bed next to me ranked right up there with it.

"So, uh…how does this work, exactly?" I resolved to have a talk with Marvin about the sad lack of employee orientation.

His pale blue eyes widened. "Well, heck, Maxie…I thought *you* would know."

"Well," I began uncomfortably. "I'm kind of new at this. In fact, you're my first client."

Actually, now that I'd gotten over the initial shock, I thought it kind of nice that my first ghost was Jeb Taber. He'd always been a really nice guy, and I'd much rather be helping him than some creepy old man ghost I didn't know. "Maybe we can figure it out together. Let's start at the beginning…what made you wander away from Shady Waste…er, Shady Rest in the first place? You're a bright guy. You had to know it was a bad idea."

"Well, Max." He sighed, standing up to pace restlessly around my bedroom. "It's a terrible thing when a body feels like he's outlived his usefulness. Everybody needs to feel needed. If you don't, there doesn't seem to be much point in hanging around, you understand?"

I guessed I did. And I didn't even mind the pacing. It was the fact his feet weren't touching the ground that creeped me out a little.

"I worked hard all my life, Maxie. I still had a few good years left, but everybody else thought different. A man should be able to have a say in how he goes out when he doesn't seem to have much say about anything else."

I could see his point. Personally, I thought his daughter Adele, a stay at home empty-nester with a four bedroom ranch on the east side of town and plenty of money to hire some help, could have taken him in when he broke his hip, at least until he was back on his feet, instead of dumping him at Shady Waste. I mean the man was her father, for heaven's sake. But, I guess that might have put the kibosh to her regularly scheduled midweek rendezvous with the weekend greeter at Wallyworld. Oh, well, I was only here to help tie up the loose ends, right? Who am I to judge?

"Okay, I get it," I concurred with a nod. "But, Mr. Taber, you wandered off from Shady Rest in November. It's June. Where've you been all this time, off traveling or something?"

"Huh, now there's something I didn't think of! No, I was hunkered down right here in Hamilton, just waiting for the right time." Jed Taber was born and raised in Hamilton and had never ventured much beyond the county line. He looked a little sad at the idea maybe he'd missed a chance to see the world, and I kind of regretted mentioning it.

As I wasn't exactly up to speed on appropriate small talk with the living impaired, I must have looked confused.

Really, can you blame me?

"Oh, you know what I mean," Jed went on. "Right after, you know…well, a body doesn't look so good. Don't smell so good, neither. Didn't want my Adele seeing me like that. You wait a couple of months and Mother Nature takes care of things. All the nasty stuff goes away and you're left with nothing but nice, clean bones. No muss, no fuss."

"That's awfully considerate of you, Mr. Taber. But, don't you think Adele was already fairly upset when you went missing? Sometimes not knowing is worse than anything you might find."

Frankly, I could not believe I was having this conversation. Firstly, he was talking about sitting around for months watching his own corpse disintegrate like a deer carcass in the woods. Secondly, he was a ghost, and he was depending on me to take care of his unfinished business so he could go forth to the great beyond, which I fervently hoped was a step up from Marvin's bus terminal. Thirdly, he was talking about sitting around for months watching his own corpse disintegrate like a deer carcass in the woods and was a ghost depending on me to take care of his unfinished business so he could go forth to the great beyond. I was so shaken up I was mentally repeating myself.

"But, how did you know where to find me, Mr. Taber?"

He scratched his head and looked thoughtful for a minute. "Well, Max, now I don't rightly know. I was sitting out there along the river and I made up my mind it was time to go. The only thing I had left to do was let someone know where my body was. I saw a light, and then I was here. By the way, Max, those fifteen-hundred count Egyptian Cotton sheets are sure a real treat, always heard they were something special."

"Aren't they though," I began animatedly. "Denise bought them for my last birthday. I always thought they were a little over the top, but you know Denise, and honestly, once you've slept on them, nothing else will...okay, Mr. Taber...not exactly the issue right now. I guess you're going to tell me where your, uh, body is, and then I have to make sure somebody finds it, right?"

"I would sure appreciate it, Maxie. Hate to admit it, but I've been feeling a little tired lately. I'm about ready for a rest."

Speaking of tired, I was willing to bet the bags under my eyes had their own carry-ons by now. I did feel sad about Jeb Taber's death, though. When Denise and I went to his store after school as kids, he'd always sneak a couple of extra licorice whips or a handful of bubblegum into our bag of penny candy. Everyone had grieved his loss months ago. Now all that remained were the good-byes. He seemed to realize it, too.

"I'm out along River Road, right past the Bar-B-Q Hut, over the tracks, twenty feet into the woods on the right, along the river." He sighed. "I always did love fishing that spot."

"Guess that hip replacement didn't slow you down nearly as much as people thought, hmmm?" I laughed. The area he described had to be nearly ten miles from Shady Waste. "I don't think any of the search parties even considered venturing so far out. Would tomorrow be soon enough, Mr. Taber? I've had kind of a rough day."

If I went out in the woods in the middle of the night and claimed to have coincidentally stumbled onto a dead body, I'd be on my way right back to the hospital. Except this time it wouldn't be to the observation ward, it would be to the sixth floor psychiatric unit.

"That'd be fine, honey. I've waited this long, right? Not like I'm going anywhere." He patted my cheek and I was surprised to find his hand was warm. In fact, it surprised me I could feel it at all. "Thanks, Maxie, you always were a good girl."

My phone vibrated again and I realized nearly an hour had passed. I walked over to grab it and turned around to tell Jeb if he ran into a guy named Marvin, he should tell him I was looking for him. But Jeb Taber was already gone.

Chapter Four

Eight hours and as many phone calls later, Roger either reconciled himself to the fact that he would never get a word in, or decided I would live. Either way, he stopped calling. My neck and shoulders were stiff and sore, but happily the crowd in my head had given up the conga line in favor of a slow, rhythmic rhumba.

I still had no idea how to resolve the matter of Jed Taber's remains. The location he'd indicated was several miles south of town, along the river, and halfway into the woods. It wasn't an area I usually frequented. Okay, it wasn't an area I ever frequented, though I did like a good pork barbecue with pickle relish from the Bar-B-Q Hut every now and again.

I couldn't think of a single plausible reason to be there traipsing through the underbrush. How could I possibly explain being somewhere I had no reason to be and oh, by the way, I just happened to find a body while hanging around there? I personally never had much of an interest in bones and anthropology. The skeletal remains in the Museum of Natural History had creeped me right out during my first and only visit on a high school field trip. I didn't think I would be any more impressed, or find it any less creepy, to discover skeletal remains out in the woods. Even if I already knew they were there. Even if I'd chatted with the owner only last night. Even if I knew that Jeb had moved on to somewhere else and the bones were nothing more than bones.

I thought this might be a good time to at least sneak a look at that book of Marvin's, prior to attempting any spiritual interventions. Wasn't that what he'd advised me to do? I still felt annoyed that Marvin hadn't been decent enough to allow me enough time to attend to my fatal head injury, get a good night's sleep, and actually have a chance to read the book before he'd directed the first client my way. Of course, I didn't know what his schedule was looking like today. You know what they say, a good boss knows how to delegate. I could understand if he'd been overwhelmed with his own work, what with the big crowd I'd seen vying for his attention yesterday.

An hour or so to work the tangles and dried blood out of my hair would also have been appreciated. I'd done the best I could, but the effect was negligible. If anyone was rude enough to ask, I planned to tell them dragged-through-the-hedges-backwards was exactly the look I intended rocking today. I padded into the bedroom and retrieved the book from my nightstand along with my phone, hoping for some answers, or at least a few helpful hints, legitimate suggestions, or otherwise useful allusions. I grabbed my coffee cup from the island and transferred it to the end table, curled up at the end of the sofa, and prepared to be enlightened.

The waiver Marvin said I was required to sign was right there on page one, so I figured I should probably get it out of the way first. I dug around in the drawer of the table, pushing aside the assortment of dry rotted rubber bands, half spent packs of matches, and last year's telephone book until I finally came up with a pen that would actually write. Then I jammed everything back in and closed the drawer. I should probably have tossed half of it in the trash, but I didn't have it in me. You never knew when something would come in handy. Actually, I did know—it would come in handy or be desperately needed about five minutes after I threw it away. So, I didn't. Simpler that way, though storage does become a problem. One more reason OCD Stepmother and I had clashed when I still lived at home. To this day, I cannot get her to understand the rationale behind hoarding.

I folded back the brown leather cover and began to read. A girl should never sign anything without reading it. Just saying.

Waiver/Release for Responsibility

I _____ understand and agree to assume the duties of the Superintendent of Spiritual Intervention (SSI) for the time period specified by the Office of Central Processing,(OCP) a subsidiary of Grim Reapers Local 777. I further understand that the Office of Central Processing (OCP) is not responsible for any service, repair, maintenance, or damage to any of my personal property or professional equipment, up to and including my physical body that may occur while carrying out said duties.

I personally assume all risks in connection with this position and will not hold the Office of Central Processing, (OCP) its agents or employees liable for any injury or damage that may occur as a result. I release the Office of Central Processing, (OCP) its agents and employees, of responsibility for any harm, foreseen or unforeseen, that may arise, and further indemnify and hold harmless the Office of Central Processing, (OCP) its agents and employees from any claim or action by me or my family, estate, heirs or assigns, arising out of my assumption of said duties.

I further state that I am of legal age and am competent to sign this release; that I understand the terms are contractual; and that I have signed this document as my own free act. I have fully informed myself of the contents of this release by reading it before I signed it, and am familiar with its contents.

Well, it appeared the Office of Central Processing (OCP) had read the latest edition of the Cover Your Ass (CYA) manual from cover to cover before they'd drafted this baby. It bothered me a little no specific time frame seemed to be indicated, but Marvin and I had a verbal agreement I would take the job only until the real SSI was back. A verbal agreement held up as well as a written contract in a court of law, right? Judge Julie said so. And who would want to mess with *her*?

Swallowing my misgivings, said misgivings being if I didn't keep up my end of the bargain I'd be whisked back to an orange plastic chair at bus stop hell. At that point, it occurred to me I wasn't exactly sure what my end of the bargain was. I'd promised to fill in for the SSI, but what if I screwed up? What if I was no better than Buddy? Oh well, what did I have to lose? Oh, that's right, maybe my life. I signed with a flourish, took a sip of coffee, and flipped to page one.

The page was blank, as were the next twenty-five. Swallowing the sick sort of panic rising in my throat, I continued to flip, flip, flip, until, with a sigh of relief, I saw the bold, dark print on page twenty-six directing me to refer to Appendix A. I quickly flipped through more blank pages until I found the one labeled Appendix A in a beautifully scrolled calligraphy. All right! Now we're talking! I took a deep breath and turned the page.

Life and Death are much the same.
Neither comes with an instruction manual.
Good luck.
M.

That's it? That's what I get? Seriously? They were the only two pages that weren't blank in the entire book, except for the waiver I'd already signed. That's when I realized it was entirely possible Marvin had screwed me. Royally. Then again, on the upside, it shouldn't take long to memorize. Glass half full, Max, glass half full.

I tossed the book aside.

Okay, if you really must know, I threw it across the room with a great deal of force and a couple of choice words I haven't used in years. Well, not since the night at Alberto's, anyway.

Caesar simply picked up his head, blinked, yawned, and went back to sleep. If it didn't involve belly rubs, kitty treats, or catnip, it simply was beyond his sphere of interest. I spent a few minutes hyperventilating as I wondered how I was supposed to do this with no direction at all, when it occurred to me Buddy might be able to help. Okay, so I'd had him suspended, but honestly, who could blame me? It was his fault I was in this mess in the first place. The little weasel owed me, right?

My yellow carbon copy discharge instructions suggested I shouldn't drive. They did not, however, say I *couldn't* drive. I am one of those people who process directions in very concrete terms when it suits my purpose. It's all in the interpretation. That's my story and I'm sticking to it. I grabbed my purse, dropped my phone inside, and donned my sunglasses. In my haste, I almost ran headfirst into my father who was at the top of my steps reaching for the door while juggling a covered casserole dish and a juice pitcher.

"Whoa," he yelled, artfully keeping the casserole from pitching over the railing. "Where do you think you're going?"

"I uh, need to run down to the SuperSave," I replied, grabbing for the casserole. "I'm out of orange ju…" I spied the pitcher of juice and grabbed it, then I stepped back inside to put it in the fridge. "Toilet paper. I'm out of toilet paper." Quick thinking, huh? Dad shuffled in behind me and slid the casserole onto the island.

"What's all this?" I lifted the foil and saw a bowl of oatmeal and a couple of slices of buttered raisin toast. It had been my favorite comfort food whenever I'd been sick as a child. Something heavy and uncomfortable settled in my chest. It might have been emotion, it might have been gratitude. Then again, it might have been the antibiotics.

"Well, Gail thought you might not feel up to cooking so she made you something in case you were hungry." I pondered that for a moment. I guess I had been keeping more of a distance than I realized. Apparently Gail thinks I cook. Seriously? It's not that I can't, but since the divorce, I simply don't. "She would have brought it over herself, but, well her eyes are still kind of puffy, and since I was on my way out to work I said I'd bring it." He took me by the shoulders and turned me around to get a view of the back of my head. "Wanted to see how you were doing, anyway. Nice hair."

"Thanks, it's all the rage this season. I'm stiff and sore, but the headache isn't too bad this morning. I'm pretty sure I'll live." Assuming I could figure out this whole SSI thing and keep my end of the bargain. Otherwise, I wasn't quite as certain as I implied. Just one more reason to hurry down to the SuperSave and see what Buddy could tell me.

"Should you be driving? Why don't you just run next door and grab a couple of rolls? You know Gail always buys those supersize family packs. I don't know how much toilet paper she thinks two people need, but we have enough stockpiled to survive the apocalypse."

"Well, Dad, you know Gail. She thrives on organization." I laughed and the pain spiked. I swallowed a moan and kept a smile plastered on my face. If he realized I wasn't feeling quite as well as I claimed, I'd be further delayed by an argument. "Thanks for the offer, but I might see something else I need while I'm there. I'll be careful, and tell Gail I said thanks for the food." I took his arm, moving toward the door and picking up my purse as I spoke.

Sally Subtle, that's me!

"Why don't you wait till later? Your sister will be over after she drops the kids at soccer. She can take you."

"I'll be fine, Dad, really. Don't worry so much. I'm a big girl. Oh hey," I propelled him through the door and followed right behind before he had a chance to protest. "Tell Gail I said thanks for cleaning the bathroom, too. She didn't have to do that."

"Well, she's paying for it this morning, for sure. You should tell her yourself." It wasn't what he said, but how he said it. This time it appeared he wasn't willing to be the go between.

"Um, yeah...you're probably right. I should. I mean, yeah, I will." I would have laughed at the look of astonishment on his face at my easy capitulation and complete lack of sarcasm, but I knew it would make my head hurt. "See you later, Daddy. Have fun hawking hardware."

I stretched up and kissed his cheek as we parted ways at the foot of the stairs, he to his truck and me to my car. It was still parked at the curb from when I'd come home yesterday. Though still early, the temperature and humidity were already climbing, and I left the windows open while the AC struggled to do battle with the heat. The wind whipping through the open windows only enhanced my already dubious hairdo and I was glad when the cool air finally started pouring out of the vents and I could roll them up.

The parking lot at the SuperSave was already half filled even at this hour. It was the only real supermarket in town, so everyone did most of their basic shopping here for lack of a convenient alternative. I squeezed my little car between a battered minivan and a mud covered pickup with over-sized tires and a Confederate flag sporting a bumper sticker that read "If the mud ain't a flyin' you just ain't a tryin!" I wondered if there were any comedians in town. I was pretty sure I'd found them a redneck joke.

I didn't really need toilet paper, but I felt compelled to buy something, so I grabbed a four pack of my favorite brand anyway, the soft kind with quilting which never, ever had the poor taste to stick to your bottom no matter what it was called upon to absorb. I figured with all of the coffee Gail and Denise were stockpiling next door, it probably wouldn't hurt to pick up an extra carton of heavy cream. Upon further consideration, I switched it for a carton of Half and Half, instead. A girl has to cut back somewhere. Well, except for Denise, who seems to have gotten not only the looks in the family, but also the monopoly on metabolism.

Thus limping along with my little red basket, I headed for the checkout to confront Buddy. There were four registers open, each with a moderate line. I scanned the checkout area and didn't see Buddy anywhere. I did, however, see Bag Boy and so I got in his line, even though it was the longest. Not only was it the longest, it was apparently a magnet for every coupon clipper this side of the Appalachians. With time on my hands, I continued to scan the area for Buddy, without success. When I finally reached the register, I waited until I'd been rung up and bagged.

"Is Buddy working today?" I asked Bag Boy. Now that I bothered to take a gander at his red polyester vest, I could see his name was actually George.

"Who?" He blinked blankly.

"Buddy. You know, the kid that was here yesterday. He worked the register and you were bagging. Blond highlights, purple braces, big thick glasses. Buddy."

"Sorry, lady, I don't know who you're talking about. I don't know any guy named Buddy."

"Sure you do," I insisted exactly the way my ex-mother-in-law used to.

"You remember Mrs. Clarke?"

"No, I don't."

"Sure, you do." It had always driven me crazy.

"You were working on his line yesterday. I bought hair color. He called me ma'am. I was not happy. That Buddy, remember?"

George started to appear more nervous every second. Maybe it was the crazed look in my eyes and the Medusa hair. Maybe it had something to do with the way I pointed my finger at him, mere millimeters away from poking his eye out. Maybe the way I maniacally clutched my toilet paper made me appear desperate to hurt something. Whatever it was, he shrugged and shook his head as he made a covert move to put the counter between us. Self-preservation is an admirable quality. "Anybody here know a guy named Buddy?" he called out to the others. A great deal of shrugging and head shaking ensued, but no one owned up.

"Look, George, I came in here yesterday. You were here yesterday. Buddy was here yesterday. I really need to talk to him. I understand if you can't tell me where he lives or give me his number or anything, but can you at least give him a message for me?"

"Look, lady, I don't know who you're talking about and I don't know no Buddy," he insisted stubbornly.

"You know what, George? I forgot to take my happy pills today and I'm all out of sunshine and rainbows, okay? I want to talk to a manager." George looked past me, over my shoulder, and I realized I wouldn't have to wait very long to do precisely that.

I spun on my heel and found myself face to coffee stained tie and heroically straining buttons with Bob

Grubly, the Front End Manager. I've known Bob for ages. Well, at least for twenty years and fifty pounds. The twenty years were mutual, the fifty pounds were exclusively his. We'd gone to the same high school. Bob was a SuperSave success story. He started as an afterschool cashier at fifteen and now, a wife and four kids later, the first one born three months prior to our high school graduation, he'd worked his way up to Front End Manager. Go, Bob! It was rumored that to stretch the old paycheck, Bob took his meals at the SuperSave on the days he was scheduled to work, apparently in the Bakery aisle. I scientifically deduced this from the pendulous mound of adipose tissue straining to burst forth from the front of his shirt, coupled with the flecks of frosting and chocolate sprinkles still clinging to his nineteen seventies style porn-stache.

"Is there a problem here, Maxine?" He made an effort to appear authoritative by throwing back his shoulders, standing up straight, and sticking out his chest importantly. He was thwarted in the attempt by the gravitational pull of his belly and the button that popped off and nearly took out my eye.

"Morning, Bob," I began pleasantly. "How are Gerri and the kids? Everybody doing okay?"

He nodded. "Did you know Gerri went back to beauty school? Just got her license. She's working at a salon over in Beaumont," he bragged happily, then eyed my hair. "You should go over and see her. I bet she could fix you right...I mean, I'm sure you'd like her work."

I self-consciously reached up to smooth my hair, and then let my hand fall back to my side. What was the point? A weed-whacker was probably my only option at this stage.

"Bob, I'm looking for a kid named Buddy. He was working yesterday. Tall, skinny, blond streaks, purple braces, big glasses, apparently calls everyone from fifteen to fifty-five ma'am?"

He screwed up his face and tapped his chin as though lost in thought.

"You've done such a great job teaching your staff the importance of confidentiality, I admire that, really, but it's kind of urgent I speak with him, so if you could maybe give him a call and ask him to contact me as soon as possible, I'd appreciate it." I tried the coy eyelash batting thing again. It didn't hurt as much as it had last night, and was far more effective on Bob the Front End Manager than it had been on Unibrow the Boy Wonder. Of course, Bob had had a crush on me since the tenth grade.

"Gee whiz, Max."

Gee whiz? Seriously? Who says that anymore? Just one of a laundry list of reasons why Bob's tenth grade crush on me never panned out for him. Don't get me wrong, Bob is a nice enough guy, if you like the type. He loves his wife, coaches soccer and little league, and doesn't smoke or drink. I'm just not a "gee whiz" kind of girl. Of course, his marriage had survived where mine had not, so who was I to judge?

"I'd really like to help you, Max, but we don't have anyone named Buddy working here."

"Bob," I said in a strained voice intended to clearly indicate I'd reached the end of my patience. "He was here yesterday. I saw him. I talked to him. He called me ma'am."

Okay, so I was still a little fixated on the whole ma'am thing. I'm working on it.

Bob was shaking his head, porn-stache sprinkles all a-quiver. "Sorry, Max...you must have made a mistake."

No, I hadn't made a mistake, but it was clear I wasn't going to get anywhere here at the SuperSave. Marv must have taken that suspension thing pretty seriously. I wanted to scream in frustration. I wanted to beat my fists on Bob's jiggling abdomen, slap the sprinkles out of his porn-stache, stomp my feet, and demand Buddy's contact information. It might be a waste of time but at least I would feel like I was doing something productive. I was a thirty-five year old recently dead SSI orientee without a preceptor, and it looked more and more like it was going to stay that way. There was no sense taking it out on Bob. It wasn't his fault and it would only get me another mandatory stint in the anger management class it had been suggested I take after the Alberto's incident.

Suggested and sentenced mean the same thing, right?

I considered the whole thing a waste of time and I didn't have much success convincing the instructor I didn't need anger management. I needed people to stop pissing me off. She mumbled some snide comment about my ability to rationalize being the most advanced she'd ever seen. I took it as a compliment.

I patted Bob's beefy bicep. Okay, I sort of punched it, hard. But, I meant it in a friendly way and it made me feel a little less helpless.

"Thanks anyway, Bob. You have a good weekend, now, and tell Gerri I said hi." I clutched my toilet paper and double bagged Half and Half dejectedly.

"Sure, Max. Sorry I couldn't help. You have a good weekend, too." He gave his bicep a brisk rub. I know how to punch. I even know enough to keep my thumb outside so it doesn't get broken. "Hey, don't forget to sign up for the mailing list on your way out...lots of good coupons." He winked.

I raised a hand in a listless farewell, ignoring the stares of cashiers and customers alike, as I picked my way through the obstacle course of carts and baggers, and beat a hasty retreat. Since I only had the two items, I didn't bother to open the trunk. I propped the double bagged Half and Half on the passenger seat and secured it in place with my purse in the event it decided to tip over and leak. There is nothing worse than the smell of soured dairy products in a hot car. I tossed the four pack of toilet paper on the floor where it found a comfortable spot snuggled like an old friend among the castoff Hastykake wrappers and crumpled ATM receipts.

I made myself a vow to clean the car tomorrow. I make it almost every week, but when the time comes I always decide it really isn't necessary. I used to be more conscientious about car hygiene, but since I'm always the sole occupant these days, it doesn't seem to matter one way or the other. I'd forgotten to open the windows before I went into the store, so I propped open the door and held it with my foot to let some of the hot air out before turning the key and flicking on the AC switch.

Did you know experts claim the car dashboard, the optional upgraded upholstery, and even the cute little Christmas tree hanging on the rearview mirror emit Benzene? Benzene causes cancer, poisons your bones, and reduces the number of your white blood cells. Research indicates in a car parked in the sun at a temperature above sixty degrees, Benzene levels can easily exceed those considered safe. I figured since it was approaching eighty-five outside, it was a good bet I had already sailed by the safe zone. I know all this because Roger read about it a few years ago in some distinguished medical journal—or maybe it was an email chain letter—and insisted I start airing out the car before breathing. Besides the obvious danger of having your foundation melt into your blush, and the potential blinding results of having your mascara run, who knew getting into a sealed car on a hot day could be so hazardous? I already had enough problems, why take the chance?

I leaned my head back against the seat and immediately realized my mistake when the pressure on the staples made my head start to hurt again. I leaned forward to rest my forehead on the steering wheel instead, and found the position no more comfortable since it caused my neck to pull on my scalp also making my head start to hurt again. Finally, I closed the door and sat up straight staring out the windshield at the weekly specials posted in the big plate glass windows of the SuperSave. My excitement meter quivered when I noticed split chicken breasts were on sale for ninety-nine cents per pound. Mental note: alert the Grill Master.

But, I digress.

I began to fear my lifelong penchant for impulsivity had gotten me in over my head this time. True, I hadn't given the particulars of this position much thought before proposing my bargain to Marvin, but in light of my being dead at the time there had been Denial with a capital D to consider. I wasn't willing to consider Acceptance with a capital A. Not when there might be a Bargain with a capital B that I could use as a way out. So, now I had a body in the woods expecting to be discovered, an employee manual filled with blank pages, a GRIT who had gone AWOL, and four rolls of toilet paper I didn't even need. And it was only nine o'clock in the morning.

Now what?

Chapter Five

I put the car in reverse and prepared to back out of the parking spot. That required me to twist my entire upper body at the waist in a most unnatural way in order to look behind me while avoiding any painful tugs and pulls on my neck and scalp. When my cell phone jangled from the bottomless cavern of my purse, I jiggled the gearshift back into park and reached for my bag, scrounging around until I found it. It was at the bottom. Naturally.

It was Denise, and she wasn't happy.

"Where are you?" she demanded petulantly. Denise has a PhD in petulant. When she combines it with a hint of tears in her big, blue eyes and turns it full force on Brad-The-Famous-Vascular-Surgeon, it gets her almost anything she wants. Me? Nah, I'm immune to her tricks. I'd watched her go through puberty perfecting them.

"I'm right here. Where are you?" I returned pleasantly. I could hear Clinique, her Petit Basset Griffon Vendéen, howling frantically in the background. Yes, my sister named her dog after a cosmetic company. She also has two goldfish named Estee and Lauder, respectively. Have I mentioned her preoccupation with shopping? Clinique is a bit outspoken. She likes to howl. She howls alone, she howls with friends, she howls to music, she howls at being left alone. Sometimes she howls for the cheap thrill of hearing herself howl. Either that, or she howls because she knows it annoys me. She loves me. I don't know why, but she does. She's like a cat in that way. She finds the one person in the room who would just as soon avoid her like the plague and becomes their new best friend.

"I'm at Mom's. She asked me to run over and check on you. Have you seen her eyes? They're a mess! Anyway, then we noticed your car was gone. You aren't even supposed to be driving, Max. We were worried. Don't you ever think of anyone but yourself?"

"I do, actually. Dad said they were running low on toilet paper, and I knew you'd need some Half and Half with all of the coffee over there you and Gail have yet to conquer, so I took a little trip to the SuperSave. And no one said I *couldn't* drive, they said I *shouldn't* drive. Please note the difference." A moment of silence met my rebuttal while Denise tried to decide if I was being sarcastic. Sometimes it took her a couple of minutes to catch on. Finally, I almost heard her eyes roll.

"Are you on your way home?"

"Yep. Should be there in about ten minutes."

"Okay, I want to see you and make sure you're all right. I have to leave in about forty minutes because Clinique has an appointment at the groomer."

"Okay, see you in a few."

"Okay. Um, Max? You know Mom doesn't need toilet paper right? I think Dad must have been kidding around. She always has enough for an army. I think she might be a closet doomsday prepper."

I couldn't help laughing. Sometimes she got me and sometimes she didn't, but as different as we were, and as second rate as I sometimes felt in comparison, I did love my sister.

"I'll see you in a bit, Denise…bye."

****

At least Denise managed to pull all the way into the driveway today, so I was able to park alongside her near the bottom of my steps. I left the toilet paper in the car and grabbed the double bagged Half and Half. Clinique stood guard just inside the back door waiting for me. I have to admit she's cute, even if she is a little goofy looking. She is primarily white with spots of orange, lemon, and black, mostly around her head and ears. Her ears are set low and hang like fuzzy rags, and if you stretch them out—and I have when I really want to annoy her—they reach the tip of her nose. Her shaggy muzzle which, now that I considered it, reminded me a little of Bob the Front End Manager's porn-stache. With her long, tapered tail wagging incessantly, she freely voiced her pleasure at my arrival with an assertive, and unexpectedly loud, bray given her relatively petite size. Unlike Caesar, she found pleasure in my company even when I didn't come bearing food.

Gail and Denise were at the kitchen table lingering over coffee and Long Johns and I snagged one without waiting to be asked as I headed to the fridge to deposit the Half and Half. There is just something about the taste of raspberry jam wrapped in a freshly fried doughnut, topped with thick white frosting and coconut that makes the whole day seem brighter. My day, at least. Of course, it also makes the hips seem bigger. I guess everything worthwhile requires sacrifice. Gail had a cold washcloth pressed to her eyes and Denise hopped up to pop in a cartridge of coffee for me.

"Espresso or French Roast?" Denise was well-acquainted with my addiction to the hard stuff.

"Espresso," I mumbled through my mouthful of bakery delight as I pulled out a chair and sat down. Gail lowered the cloth then, and it became obvious she was in misery. Her eyes were red and angry looking, and Dad hadn't been kidding when he said they were still a little puffy. They were still a lot puffy. Denise plunked a steaming mug laced with exactly the right amount of Half and Half in front of me and resumed her seat across the table.

"Hey Gail, um, thanks for cleaning the bathroom last night," I said after washing down my bite of pastry with a swig of java. "You should have left it. You look worse than I feel."

"You're welcome, Max. It was no trouble. It looks worse than it is. The itching and burning have let up this morning and my sinuses are clear... It's just that the swelling doesn't seem to want to go down."

"Yeah, it *was* a lot of trouble. It was a mess in there. Plus you're so allergic to Caesar that I'm sure you had a hell of a night. I appreciate it." The truth is, I probably wouldn't have done it for her and with the way I'd been acting, I guess it said something that she'd done it for me.

"Did the alarm clock and oven timer wake you up okay?" she asked. "I was going to call and check on you, but I doubled up on the antihistamine and it knocked me for a loop."

"Actually, I turned them off. Roger felt compelled to call me every hour on the hour to make sure I was still breathing, so it turns out they weren't necessary after all." Gail and Denise exchanged a look but thankfully, made no comment "That swelling looks nasty. Have you tried hemorrhoid cream?"

Gail nearly spit her coffee across the table. "No...um..." She coughed. "What would make you suggest I try that?"

"Well, Mom, she *was* married to a proctologist for thirteen years," Denise giggled. Since I rarely missed an opportunity to take a shot at Brad-the-Famous-Vascular-Surgeon's socks, I guess I deserved it.

"Actually, it's an old trick models and actresses use to reduce under-eye puffiness," I grinned.

"Well, since the last time I checked, it looked like I do have hemorrhoids under my eyes, I guess Roger would probably have made the same recommendation." Gail chuckled, surprising me. Who knew she and I had a similar sense of humor? "Well, we don't have any anyway," she continued. "That's one ailment of advanced years both your father and I have managed to avoid so far. Maybe I'll try some cold tea later... It seems to work for most anything. Remember the summer we went to the Jersey Shore? Max, you were about twelve, I think, and Denise must have been about four."

"Oh my God, you had such a crush on that lifeguard, Max, remember? What was his name? Tad...Todd?" Denise asked.

"Rod," I groaned in mortified recollection. "His name was Rod." I was twelve and he was eighteen, and I thought he hung the moon. I mistook politeness on his part for reciprocation of my pie-eyed adoration and planted myself on the beach outside our rental house in my new, blue leather-look two piece for hours, confidently waiting for him to walk by and realize I was the girl of his dreams. I also slathered my skin in some delicious coconut scented orange gel with an SPF 0 that makes you feel tan as soon as you rub it on.

I fried like a pan full of pork rinds in bacon grease. My eyes swelled shut, I could barely walk, and angry, pus filled blisters popped up all over my legs. While my dad amused Denise, Gail made a huge pot of tea, cooled it down with trays of ice cubes, and tore a cotton sheet into strips. She spent the last three days and nights of our seven day vacation at my bedside putting the soothing, tea soaked compresses on my damaged skin, replacing them as they took on the heat of the burn, and forcing me to drink lots of fluids. In retrospect, she couldn't have gotten much sleep, and I guess it wasn't much of a vacation for her, either. At the time, I could only think Rod was surely now lost to me forever. But, somehow, everything felt so much better when Gail applied the compresses. I'd forgotten.

"To this day, my calves won't take a tan." I laughed.

"I'm not surprised," Gail concurred. "I'm shocked you ever went out in the sun again after that!"

I stuffed the remainder of my Long John in my pie-hole, got up from the table, and pulled a big saucepan from the overhead rack. I filled it with water and put it on the stove, turning the flame up to high. Clinique, who had been curled around my feet, suddenly made a dash for the back door and set up howling again.

"What are you doing?" Denise shouted over the din.

"Making tea." I caught Gail's eye and saw her swallow hard.

Then she smiled. "Thanks," she said.

I shrugged. "What is wrong with that crazy animal?"

"Oh, she probably smells a rabbit or squirrel or something. If she gets a whiff of something, forget it. She's a good dog, and the kids adore her, but scent trumps obedience every time!" Denise laughed. "Clinique, stop!"

But Clinique was on overdrive and was running like a rabid racehorse from the front door to the back in a long oval, crashing into the walls as she tried to make the turns and sliding across the hardwood floors, pushing all of Gail's throw rugs into wrinkled piles in the process.

"When she gets wind of a scent, you can't even hold her on the leash. That's why we put the fence up behind the pool. She can run around all she wants and we don't have to risk walking her on the street for her to get exercise."

I tossed a handful of teabags into the boiling water and retrieved the washcloth Gail had dropped on the table. I turned the heat down to let the tea steep for a while and filled a bowl with ice cubes from the ice maker on the door of the fridge.

Denise had finally managed to grab Clinique's collar on one of her pass-bys and clipped the leash in place. "I'm going to drop her at the groomer's and then while they're dealing with *her* fur, I'm coming back to deal with *yours*." She looked pointedly at my head.

"Oh, I don't know, Denise," I hedged as I fished out the teabags with a slotted spoon and added the ice. "My head is pretty sore. Maybe we should leave well enough alone for a day or two."

"It'll be twice as hard to deal with in a day or two. You can't see back there and I can. I'll be careful, and you'll feel better. God knows, you'll look better. Then again, you couldn't look much worse. Did you actually leave the house like that?"

I didn't bother to answer, but I did stick my tongue out and we all laughed. "What time do you have to pick Clinique up?" I asked casually.

"About eleven thirty, why?"

"You know what I've been dying for? A pork barbecue with sweet pickle relish. Maybe I'll go with you when you pick her up. Your mom can lie down and rest for a while with her tea rag on, and you and I can drive out to the Bar-B-Q Hut and bring back lunch. Gail, this tea is going to stain. Do you have an old cloth you don't care about?"

"Oh, that one's fine, Max. Don't worry about it. You girls don't have to get take out, I could make something here," Gail protested.

"You've had a long night, too. You feel like crap, you look like crap, and you cleaned my bathroom at great personal sacrifice. Let me take care of lunch. I'm dying for a barbecue. So what'll it be? Ham or pork?"

"Well, if you're sure," Gail said uncertainly. "It isn't any trouble at all for me to…"

I slapped the tea soaked cloth across her eyes. "Ham or pork?"

"Ham," she yelped as the cold cloth hit her square in the face. "And maybe you could get me some of those French Fried Onion rings, too? I mean as long as you're going."

"Sure." Yeah, I had an ulterior motive, but all things considered, taking care of lunch probably was the least I could do. I guess being dead made you think about things like how someone might remember you. My behavior up until now certainly didn't guarantee I'd be remembered fondly.

Just saying.

Denise returned from taking Clinique to the groomer with a bottle of spray-in conditioner—from the pharmacy, not the groomer. True to her word she was careful and meticulous and gently worked through every tangle, one at a time. She kept up a running commentary on the kids' latest activities, and we both laughed at her confession about hiding Brad-The-Famous-Vascular-Surgeon's black cashmere socks, one pair at a time, and replacing them with something a little trendier. Gee, maybe she did listen to my opinion on some things. He hadn't mentioned it, but so far, he hadn't taken the hint and was still wearing the black.

You may recall it's June. Yep, sandal season.

Then she helped me wash my hair with lukewarm water while hanging upside down over the bathroom sink, using a paper cup to rinse the shampoo and keep it away from the wound. When we finished, she combed her fingers through it with the hair dryer set to cool until it was barely damp and the ends curled under. She was right. I did feel better. Much better. And I did look better. In fact, when she was finished, I looked even better than usual. She had a knack with hair, who knew? It was the probably most uninterrupted time we'd spent together since we were teenagers, before college and husbands and kids. I was surprised to realize I'd hardly felt a single twinge of jealousy the entire time.

After settling Gail on the recliner in the family

room, tea rag plastered to her eyes, TV remote and cordless phone at her fingertips, Denise and I made a pit stop at the groomer to pick up Clinique and went barreling down route ninety-two on our way to the Bar-B-Q Hut. I may have slightly exaggerated my craving for the pork barbecue with sweet pickle relish. Truth be known, while I enjoyed one every now and then, it wasn't the sort of thing I got regular cravings for. But it was the only excuse I could think of. If this didn't work, I wasn't sure how I was going to take care of Jeb Taber's unfinished business.

It was cooler along the river, the sun's heat filtered in lacework patterns through the trees overhanging the road on both sides. Of course, it might have felt cooler because Denise's luxury car boasted individual climate control for each passenger, but the dappled shade even looked more refreshing than the glaring sun in town. Yellow birch, red maples, and pitch pines scrambled for footing, their arms wrapped around granite cliffs and jutting ledges, on the rocky mountain cut to our right. Silver maple and choke cherry vied for dominance beyond the tracks and down to the water on the river side, while white birch bowed over the water lapping at the bank. Here and there a thick, succulent Rhododendron, with fuchsia flowers nearly shed, huddled in the damp coolness at their feet, moss wrapped around their roots like a verdant blanket. The river itself meandered beside the road beyond the trees, reflecting the sun and winking invitingly through the gaps in the foliage as it raced along to the south draining nearly half of the land area of Pennsylvania into the Chesapeake and right on out to the Atlantic.

Train tracks ran parallel to the river for miles,

rusted and overgrown, reminders of Hamilton's heyday when coal was king. Downtown, the Gilded Age mansions of the coal barons, now subdivided into multi-family apartments, trendy shops, and college dorms—because who could afford to heat those things in this day and age—testified to an era of wealth and opulence, for the few, anyway. Out here, away from the town center, were the remnants of the hard lives of the mine workers, the years of hardship and economic decline visible in the ramshackle remains of company houses, and stray, abandoned railroad cars overgrown with coverlets of milkweed and Queen Anne's Lace.

Just outside the city limits, one solitary breaker kept silent vigil, where once there had been many. Bent and broken, its former glory was now clothed in a comic party dress of bright graffiti and encroaching forest, its arthritic bones of aged steel diseased with time and dissolution. Once it had been worshiped as an altar of industry. Now it was nothing but a creaking relic, a guardian angel of rusting works and broken glass that had become a haven for the rasping breath and heavy boots of switchblade lovers, swilling beer and panting over unsuspecting virgins.

The air was thick with history here along the river, and much of it was sad. But here, too, were the stories of those who had overcome, those who came to this country with little besides the clothes on their back and the will to succeed. They worked hard and earned little, but they were hardy and determined. They scrimped and they saved and they learned the language and taught their children the value of education. Almost everyone in town could claim a coal miner somewhere in their ancestral tree. The Logans were no exception.

Clinique lay curled up in my lap, exhausted from her battle with the groomer, filling the car with a clean puppy powder scent. She isn't a Great Dane by any means, but she also isn't the pocket-sized lapdog she thinks she is. When she saw me waiting in the passenger seat she wanted no part of sitting in the back, no matter what Denise or I said.

Did I mention she loves me?

"Max," Denise interrupted the mellow music emanating quietly from the surround sound. "Do you think Mom's okay? I mean, have you noticed anything different about her lately?"

I turned to look at her, but most of her expression was hidden behind her sunglasses.

"Different in what way? To be honest, I don't see very much of her."

"I don't know, she seems kind of quiet and distant, like maybe something is bothering her. Has she said anything to you?"

"Oh, as if! Who can you think of that your mother would be less likely to confide in than me?"

Denise shrugged. "I don't know, it seemed like you were getting along okay today."

"Well, I have to admit I was touched she'd saved all my mom's things for me. I have to give her a few brownie points for that, I guess."

"I thought you might," Denise said smugly. Too smugly.

"You knew!" I accused. "You knew about the furniture and you never said a word! That's why you started the whole redecorating nonsense. So I would figure it out. You never had any intention of buying me a sofa, did you? You are nothing but a well-shod and devious wench."

"I promised I wouldn't say anything. Mom didn't want you to feel obligated to thank her or make a big deal about it. I figured out you didn't even remember the stuff. I told Mom you were too young at the time to recognize it. Heck, you were only six or seven when your mom passed, weren't you?"

"Just turned six. I can't believe I didn't realize it sooner. Guess I repressed more than I thought from back then," I mused.

"Maybe," Denise agreed slowly. "Or maybe you haven't repressed it at all, maybe you unconsciously pick and choose what you care to remember and how you care to remember it."

"What do you mean?" I asked warily. Denise shrugged and didn't answer. She put on her blinker, and after waiting for a slow moving semi to go by in the other lane, made a sweeping turn into the dirt patch in front of the Bar-B-Q Hut that passed for a parking lot. Even though it was lunch time, business didn't usually pick up until later when people headed out of town after work and stopped in to pick up a quick dinner or chat with the regulars who made it their business to hang out until closing every night of the week.

Have I mentioned this is a small town?

Denise slid her sunglasses to the top of her head and reached around into the back seat to grab her bag.

"Denise, what did you mean when you said I pick and choose what I remember and how I remember it?"

"Nothing."

"Denise."

Denise took a deep breath and then let it out as if considering how, or whether, to answer. She turned in her seat and looked at me with an earnestness I'm not sure I've ever seen on her face. "Max, you're my sister and I love you. You're smart and you're funny, but sometimes it's been quite a challenge for me trying to live up to you."

I opened my mouth to tell her *she* was the one who was hard to live up to, *she* was the one everyone thought was perfect and beautiful. I was sloppy seconds. I just happened to have been born first. But, before I could get the words out, she gave me a talk-to-the-hand-gesture.

"Please, Max, let me get this out. I probably should just keep my big mouth shut and leave well enough alone, but today, at the house…well, it was *nice*. You weren't throwing digs at my mom and she wasn't bending over backwards trying to please you. You were actually nice to her, and guess what? It didn't kill you. I know you think she loves me more because she's *my* mother and not yours. Guess again, Max. You may not consider her your mother, but she does. She always has. You think about it really hard. Anything she would do for me she would do for you. More so in fact, because she always tries harder with you. You should have heard her when she called me last night. She was so upset I thought you actually died, or something. You think she would have cleaned my bathroom last night if I had a cat? I wish she cut me half the slack she cuts you. You, apparently, can do no wrong when it comes to my mother. Somehow, I never quite measure up."

She stopped talking to dig a tissue out of her purse while I simply stared at her incredulously. In fact, I was rendered momentarily speechless, no mean feat.

"I'm sorry, Max, I shouldn't have said anything. I

sure didn't have this big heart to heart on my agenda today, especially in the parking lot of the Bar-B-Q Hut of all places, but I'm worried about her and I'm worried about you. You've changed. I don't know what it is, but your attitude is like a barbed wire fence sometimes. You wrap yourself up in it and it's so sharp and painful it pushes the people who love you away, even when they try to get past it. And then you resent them for it. I miss you. Today it felt like I had my sister back, and I liked it. And now I've probably gone and ruined everything by opening my big yap." She paused to blow her nose. "And on top of everything, Brad is still wearing those damn black socks no matter what I do."

And then I laughed because I realized it was exactly the kind of one liner I might have used to break the tension and avoid becoming too maudlin. I looked into those big, blue eyes swimming with unshed tears and I knew it wasn't the fake waterworks she used to get her way with Brad-the-Famous-Vascular-Surgeon.

Although, it apparently hadn't worked on him with the socks. I'd have to give it some more thought. Maybe I should tell her to hide the sandals?

She actually believed she had to try harder than I did with Gail? I had to acknowledge some of what she said might be true. Gail probably would not have cleaned her bathroom last night if she had a cat. Then again, Denise has people for that. Denise has people for most everything.

It actually *had* been a long time since Denise and I had spent any real time together. If I was honest with myself, I missed her, too. It wasn't her fault she led a charmed life. Okay, scratch that. It wasn't her fault *I* felt like she led a charmed life. Sometimes the ones we love most are the ones who need to be kicked in the ass the hardest. It was good to know my sister loved me enough to kick me in the ass, even if those pointy shoes of hers really hurt.

When did my little blonde sister get so smart? But, I don't know what attitude she's referring to. I don't have an attitude, I merely have a personality some people apparently cannot handle. It's a great defense mechanism. I guess I'd never considered it might be working twice as well on offense.

Hmm, imagine that—a twofer.

"Have you been dabbling in those psychology classes at the community college again, Denise? I refuse to be your case study," I frowned and thumbed away a stray tear that had managed to squeeze from the corner of her eye and work its way down to her chin.

She gave me a watery grin. "God, forbid! I have a feeling your head would be a particularly scary place to spend much time." She laughed. "You're not mad at me, are you? Are we okay?"

"Yeah, we're okay," I assured her. Although since she'd waited this long to speak her mind, it might have been nice if she waited a little longer to start in on me, at least until I had a chance to recover from my death and the residual concussion. Speaking of which, I was here on business and I'd better get to it. "Now, go and get the food while Clinique and I go hunting silly wabbits. I'll bet she has to pee by now, and she is not using my lap as her own personal doggie throne."

Clinique heard her name, rabbit, and pee all in the same sentence, and the excitement in the vehicle became palpable. She stopped just short of doing backflips to follow Denise out of the truck. Then she realized I had the leash and made a mad dash across my lap for my door as soon as my fingers touched the handle. I wrapped the leash around my wrist and held on for dear life. Clinique launched herself like a furry rocket as soon as I opened the door. She picked up her head and scented the breeze, straining against the leash. She actually had amazing strength for such a little ball of fluff. Then she pulled me right toward the tracks, past the Bar-B-Q Hut, heading toward the underbrush and the river, and hopefully toward my first successful assignment as the temporary Superintendent of Spiritual Intervention.

Chapter Six

About three steps over the tracks, I realized flip flops and cutoffs were probably not the wisest fashion choice for being dragged through the underbrush by a Petit Basset Griffon Vendéen on a mission. Weeds and brambles do not look quite as thick and impenetrable from a distance. It's all about perspective. Who knew? For the record, I am not a woodsy kind of girl. My idea of camping is a forty foot motorhome with hot running water and AC. And cable. Parked next to a restaurant and bar.

I took advantage of Clinique's momentary preoccupation with a particularly gnarled and protruding root ball to free my wrist from the wrapped leash cutting off the circulation to my right hand and pluck some shockingly sharp twigs from between my toes. I absently noted a pedicure might be in order. I was genetically cursed with my father's feet. They were not pretty.

Clinique, with her especially keen Petit Basset Griffon Vendéen senses, felt the slack in the leash immediately and before I could blink, she gave a mighty Petit Basset Griffon Vendéen leap and was off and running toward the river in hot pursuit of the silly wabbit she'd actually succeeded in startling out of its cover, dragging the leash behind her. Okay, that was not part of the plan. Denise was going to kill me.

"Clinique," I shouted. "You come back here this instant! Come on…here girl." I pushed aside the branches of the nearest shrub. The leaves were hairy and tickled my arm. I could see the bushes moving ahead, and caught sight of Clinique's furry butt wiggling in the air as it went up and over, disappearing again behind a fallen log near the water's edge.

"Max?" Denise and her kitten heels sounded faint and faraway, safely ensconced back beyond the tracks in the dusty parking lot. "Are you okay?"

"I'm fine," I called, gasping as a low hanging branch of a limber sapling snapped back to slap me in the face. "The dog got loose."

"Damn. Well, come on out of there. I'll get her."

"Oh, yeah, you'll get really far in those shoes."

"Won't need to," she called back. "Come on out." I was quite happy to turn around and make my way back to the relative civilization of the parking lot. My legs were stinging from a myriad of scrapes and scratches, and my right arm itched like crazy. Well, this had been a spectacular failure. I was going to have to move on to Plan B, as soon as I came up with a Plan B. I tripped my way over the tracks and stumbled onto the edge of the dirt lot.

"Watch and learn," my sister smirked. She loudly shook and rattled the paper Bar-B-Q Hut bag, grease spots notwithstanding. "Clinique, look what Mommy has," she called loudly, rattling the bag all the while. "Popcorn, Clinique…come on girl, popcorn." Unbelievably, after a few seconds, the bushes began to vibrate madly and out popped a familiar, long-eared, furry face. Denise kept the bag crackling, and Clinique trotted in our direction, tail in the air wagging proudly.

Clamped in her jaw was a long, white stick. She jogged happily over to Denise, dropped the stick at her feet, and looked up at my sister expectantly as if to say *where the hell is my popcorn?*

Denise's horrified gaze fixed on the gift Clinique had so proudly presented.

"Oh, my God...is that..." she began, the color in her cheeks fading from perfectly applied summer rose to an odd shade of gray-green that didn't compliment her skin tone at all.

"Sure looks like it," I answered, trying to appear equally horrified and keep my excitement in check.

It was a tibia. Not just any tibia, a human tibia. How did I know this? Have I mentioned I was in nursing school when Roger and I met? No? I dropped out when Roger and I got married, and I began working in his office. It was simply too hard to keep up with the classes and besides, I was *in lurve* and wanted to spend as much time with Roger as possible. Sure, I could finish my degree and pursue that avenue of employment now, but then I'd be working at the very same hospital as Roger. You may not see a problem with that, but let me point out once again that Hamilton is a small town. Rule number one about small towns: if you don't remember your business, just ask the neighbor...they'll know.

But, I digress. I did it! I did it! Yay me!

Well, okay, Clinique did it, but under my expert Superintendent of Spiritual Intervention supervision. Sort of. I guess I should have been as distressed at this evidence of human remains as my sister appeared to be, but all I could think of was I had actually helped bring Jeb Taber's Excellent Adventure to an end. I hoped, wherever he'd moved on to, someone made him feel needed.

"Put in a good word for me, Mr. Taber," I whispered, reaching down to grab the end of Clinique's leash to prevent it from becoming tangled around what little remained of old Jeb. I thought I felt warmth and the slight pressure of a hand on my shoulder, but when I looked up, Denise and I were the still the only ones there.

"What did you say?" she asked faintly. She was frozen in place, staring at the petrified limb gleaming in the sunlight.

"Nothing, just talking to myself." I put an arm around her shoulders and made her take a step back from Jeb's leg bone. "We should probably call someone."

She seemed to shake it off and come to herself. "Oh, yeah...that's probably a good idea." Her color slowly returned as she took the leash out of my hand and led Clinique to the car. She opened the back door and waited until the dog jumped inside. Then she started the engine, opened all of the windows a few inches for air, and tossed the bag of food on the front seat. She slammed the door and pulled her cell from her purse, punching in 911 as she walked back in my direction.

****

The arrival of the sheriff's black and white sedan with sirens blaring, followed closely by a paramedic unit, three other police vehicles, and the somber, hearse—um, okay it's a black nineteen ninety-four station wagon—driven by Ewald Grady, the county coroner, caught the attention of the other occupants of the Bar-B-Q Hut. Within minutes, the dry, dusty, dirt lot had taken on a carnival atmosphere. An enterprising SPD officer had already erected a yellow crime scene-taped perimeter around the lonely tibia and now looped his way through the trees and bushes on the other side of the tracks. An excited shout echoed from the water's edge and officers and coroner alike went crashing through the underbrush in the general direction of the fallen log.

Denise and I leaned against her vehicle, baking in the afternoon sun, and keeping our distance from the knot of Bar-B-Q Hut onlookers buzzing with curiosity. The owner thoughtfully produced a Styrofoam bowl of water for Clinique, and at last she'd stopped howling and curled up on a blanket in the back seat sleeping off her adventure. After calling Gail to tell her we were running a little late, but wisely omitting the reason why, Denise and I adopted a mutual silence while we waited for whatever happened next. I rummaged in the bottom of my purse and came up with a crushed, stale half a pack of cigarettes and tapped one out. Denise reached over and plucked it from my fingers.

"Aren't you worried about intermittent claudication?" I teased, after tapping out a second coffin nail for myself. Denise leaned in for a light and took a long, satisfying drag. She held it for a moment, and then blew it out in a long blue-white plume ending in a series of perfectly formed smoke rings. My sister was obviously not a cigarette virgin. Who knew?

"Did you know," she began distractedly, "scientists recently conducted a study on how women feel about their ass?" Since I'd made the snarky comment about intermittent claudication, I sensed a Roger joke in the offing. "The results were kind of surprising. Twenty percent of women think their ass is too fat, ten percent think their ass is too skinny, but the remaining seventy percent say they don't care. He may not be perfect but he's just right. They love him, and they wouldn't trade him for the world."

"Journal of the AMA?"

"Modern Housewife," she smiled back taking a final drag and grinding the butt into the dirt with the pointed toe of her strappy sling back, courteously doing the same for mine when I held it between my thumb and forefinger and used my middle finger to flick it in her direction.

"Brad's a lucky guy," I said, realizing it was true. I always thought Denise lived vicariously through herself, but maybe she used shopping to fill a void the way I used sarcasm. Who'd have thought?

"Yeah, well, if he's ever home long enough, I'll be sure to remind him." She laughed, but it didn't reach her eyes.

"Denise," I began hesitantly. I mean I was hardly the best person to be giving out marital advice. Look how well I'd done with my own. "Are you and Brad doing okay?"

"Oh, gosh, yeah." She straightened away from the car as men began tramping out of the woods. "We're fine. It's only that he works such long hours the way it is, and still he always goes in for an emergency, even if he isn't on call."

"People want the best." I said, and she nodded. "Denise, Brad adores you." It was true. I saw the way he looked at her when he thought no one noticed, like he couldn't quite believe his luck, even after eight years of marriage.

"I know he does. And I adore him too, black socks and all. I guess I feel sorry for myself now and then. I miss him."

I could appreciate that. I missed Roger, too. I missed the way his eyes crinkled when he smiled. I missed the way he could never find his car keys, especially when we were running late. I missed having someone to talk to over coffee in the morning and someone to rehash the day with over dinner in the evening. I missed having someone to hold me and make me feel safe in the middle of the night. I missed a lot of things. I missed him. At least, I did in those rare moments when I allowed myself to think about it at all, sitting alone in my apartment crying like a disgraced TV evangelist. This was not one of those moments, so I determinedly pushed all thoughts of Roger into the little lock box in my head where I kept them, and firmly slammed the lid.

I still hadn't eaten a thing today besides the Long John, and my stomach growled loudly in protest, tormented by the thick aroma of roasting meat and barbecue sauce hanging heavy in the summer air. I assumed chomping on a pork barbecue dripping with sweet pickle relish while being interrogated about the discovery of human remains might be considered slightly gauche. I draped an arm across my sister's shoulders, gave her a squeeze, and started walking us in the direction of Sheriff Henry Stoltz, who was just emerging from the underbrush.

Henry Stoltz is just past sixty-two, a time when most men look forward to retirement. A big, burly, bear of a man, Henry doesn't know how to relax, has no hobbies outside of law enforcement, and shows no signs of slowing down. His hair is as thick and dark and wiry as when he'd been elected sheriff nearly twenty years ago, and you have to look hard to find any hint of gray. He owes his broad face, high cheekbones, and long, straight nose to his Native American grandmother, and his color coordinated suits, crisp linen shirts, and funky character ties to his wife, Mamie, but his addiction to gumdrops is all his own.

Gumdrops? Yeah, I might enjoy them if they were soaked in cherry rum. He's never without a pocketful. He pops them like breath mints. I hate them. I think maybe it's a texture thing. I've never been a big fan of gelatin, either. My stomach gave another embarrassingly loud rumble. I wondered if he'd share.

"C'mon over here, kids," he called to my sister and me. Yes, kids. Even though both of us had long passed the age of consent, we would always be kids to Henry. I went all through school, from kindergarten to college, with Henry's daughter, Melanie. Yeah, Henry and I go way back. I even know Henry was born with a Mongolian blue spot, a kind of blue birthmark peculiar to certain ethnic groups. It's usually found on the upper aspect of the...er, derrière, but it also occurs on the back or shoulder sometimes. In some cultures, it's considered the mark of a Shaman. I don't know where Henry's blue spot is, trust me, I didn't ask. There are some things about people you just do not want to know.

"So," Henry boomed in a voice that was far louder than necessary. As sheriff, Henry owned a bullhorn. It was superfluous in Henry's case. He was a lot like my father in that way. "Tell me again what happened."

I quickly recounted the story of Clinique's potty

break that ended with the discovery of the tibia lying at our feet. I left out the part about my temporary position as SSI. I figured even with Henry's possible pre-disposition to mysticism, the revelation might cause more trouble than I could reasonably handle at the moment.

See, I'm getting better at controlling that whole impulsivity thing.

Henry nodded and diligently took notes while I scratched at my arm. It was getting red and starting to burn, too, and the skin felt bumpy and irregular. Henry snapped his notebook closed and tucked it back into the inside pocket of his suit jacket. I wondered how he stood it in this heat. Then he reached into another pocket and I realized he probably needed the storage space for his candy stash. Chomping happily, he glanced down to where I was rubbing at my arm and his broad face split into a knowing grin.

"Looks like you had a run in with some poison oak, Max. You must be real sensitive. The rash doesn't usually show up for at least a couple of hours. Try some calamine lotion…helps with the itch."

I looked in horror at the little fluid filled blisters popping up on my arm. Swell, just swell. Well, at least someone thought I was sensitive. I hadn't been accused of that anytime in recent memory. Death, concussion, dogs gnawing on old men's tibias, and now poison oak. It had been a banner weekend so far.

"Is it contagious?" Misery might love company, but I didn't want to share this particular gift with my sister and the girls.

"Nah. Be uncomfortable for a week or so, though. Try not to scratch." He laughed, swatting at my hand which had gone right back to the scene of the crime.

Denise dug in her purse and came up with a spray bottle. "Here." She grabbed my hand and pulled my arm toward her while spritzing away with the pocket-sized antiseptic. "The lidocaine will numb it for a while until we get home."

"I realize you're married to a doctor, but do you always carry first aid supplies in your purse?"

"Yeah, I do actually. Kids." She said as though it explained everything. I guess it did. "Henry, do you have any idea who it is?" She nodded uncomfortably toward the dusty tibia surrounded by the yellow warning tape.

"Well, we'll have to wait for the coroner to make the positive identification, but it's almost certainly Jeb Taber."

"Oh, no," Denise said softly. "Well, I guess it was inevitable, wasn't it? That's so sad. Adele will be devastated."

I wasn't so sure, but decided it was probably more diplomatic to keep it to myself.

What? I can so be diplomatic!

"Well, at least she'll have closure." It sounded like a trite and meaningless response, but what else could I say? I wished Henry would hurry up and get done with us. I was starving and I wanted to wash off my arm and take an antihistamine. It was probably contraindicated with my concussion, but to recap, I'd already died once this week, and I doubted an antihistamine was going to do me in. At the risk of losing my previous title of sensitivity—after all, I'd known the probable outcome of this little jaunt even before the sweet pickle relish had been slapped on my barbecue—I asked Henry if we could leave.

"Yeah, you girls go ahead. I know where to find you if I have any more questions. Doesn't look like there's any foul play involved, anyway. Looks like he sat down by that old log and went to sleep. Pretty cut and dried. Can't imagine what brought him all the way out here."

"Fishing," I whispered.

"What?" Henry and Denise were both staring at me.

"Oh, I, uh, mean he used to like fishing out here. He told me once."

Some deaths are natural, some not so much. I guess this was a kind of self-induced natural death. Sit down, fall asleep, and let the frigid temperature do its thing. It wouldn't be ruled a suicide, although the old guy clearly understood the consequences of walking away from Shady Waste in the dead of winter. But, that was between him and me. Everyone else would figure he'd probably gotten a little wifty and wandered away in confusion. Death by misadventure. Not so excellent after all.

"Yeah, he sure did love to fish," Henry said sadly. "Well, you girls run along. I'd appreciate it if you didn't say anything about this to anyone until we have a chance to notify the next of kin."

"Not even Mom and Dad?" Denise asked.

"Well, I guess you can tell them as long as they keep it to themselves until the official announcement is made."

"Okay, thanks Henry. It was good to see you. Tell Mel I said hello, will you?" I said, leaning up to give him a kiss on the cheek. It *was* good to see him, even if the circumstances left a lot to be desired. And I hadn't talked to Mel in ages. It occurred to me that in the last year or so, I had cut myself off from nearly everyone I was close to without ever realizing I was doing it. "Tell her I'll give her a call…soon."

"I will, honey. You two take care, now. Give my best to your folks." He waved us off and headed back in the direction of the tracks.

Denise and I climbed into the SUV which was blessedly cool compared to the heat outside, even though the AC wasn't quite as efficient when the thing sat idling for well over an hour. I dug into the Bar-B-Q Hut bag and handed my sister her now cold sandwich, sans wrapper, so she could munch on it while she drove. Denise called home before we pulled out and learned Gail had given up on us and made herself a sandwich, so I didn't feel the least bit guilty when I tore off the waxed paper wrappers and devoured both her barbecue and my own.

What? I told you I was starving.

I saved her the onion rings, though. I'm not a complete lout. Then I gathered up the trash and stuffed everything back in the bag.

Because we got back into town far behind our original schedule, Denise decided to swing by the school and pick Mick and Vick up from soccer practice. It was a little early, but it would save her a trip later. I had nowhere to be, and Gail's onion rings were already cold, so I had no objection to a pit stop. Besides, I hadn't seen the little gremlins in a while. Unlike me, they have a social life and always seem to be either coming or going.

Denise concentrated on weaving through the

downtown traffic while I took the time to have a look around. I didn't often have the chance to simply take in the scenery as I was usually the one driving, alone in my car. The buildings were old, predating the turn of the century, the twentieth, not the current one. Many of them had been redone in stucco, wrapped in aluminum sheeting, or covered with plywood siding, completely obscuring their Victorian architecture, beautiful detailing, and overall appeal. The landlords cared little about the historic aspect, but were in favor of anything that promised to make the area more tempting and bring in more business.

I'd always thought the modernization was a shame and was happy to see the Women's Auxiliary of the Hamilton Historical Society had made progress in convincing the landlords to start stripping off the newer facades, restoring the original charm, as part of the downtown revitalization project near and dear to their hearts. The main business district huddled around a central square, and now that the Auxiliary had concentrated their fundraising efforts, the square itself looked pretty spiffy, too. A small fountain tinkled in the center, and benches were artfully arranged among the planters and small trees. It was a pleasant place for families and college students to spend an afternoon, and with the influx of visitors, many of the formerly vacant storefronts around the square had begun to fill up with cafes, antique shops, and funky boutiques.

Denise pulled in to a parking spot behind the school near the practice fields, and I elected to wait in the car with Clinique while she went to retrieve the twins. Clinique, of course, planted herself on my lap again, her porn-stached muzzle poking through the open crack in the window, and howling to beat the band as she spotted Denise, with Mick and Vick in tow, headed for the vehicle. Chaos reigned for a good ten minutes as Clinique howled and Mick and Vick chattered incessantly, greeting me with sweat-sticky squeezes from their chubby, but surprisingly strong little arms.

I felt that same sharp little twitch in my chest I always felt around kids, like a knife wiggling around in there to get my attention and remind me of what I could never have. Denise struggled to pry them off of me and get them buckled into the back seat. Clinique quickly abandoned my lap to park her furry butt between the two little towheads with sweaty ringlets escaping identical ponytails and sticking moistly to their necks and bright, flushed cheeks. Denise pulled two juice boxes from a small cooler on the floor, and at last silence reigned as they stopped chattering long enough to slurp down six ounces of cool and fruity refreshment.

They were incredibly cute little girls, even if they were related to me. Though in looks they favored Brad, they had Denise's fair coloring, and occasionally I even saw a glimpse of my dad in them. Yes, my heart ached in the old, familiar way, but I also realized how much I'd missed the little imps. I used to see them more often when Roger and I were still together. Denise would sometimes drop them at my place for a few hours on Saturday afternoons to give herself a couple of uninterrupted shopping hours. Roger called it our "practice run" for the much anticipated day we would have children of our own. Of course, that was before we discovered a family probably wasn't in the cards for us. After that, seeing them only reminded me of what I would never have and it became easier and less painful to avoid them. It was one more thing I'd failed at while Denise had enjoyed a rousing success by popping out not just one, but two at a time.

Maybe Roger would have more luck with Barbara. Thing One and Thing Two could probably breast feed a third world country.

As you might have guessed, but I, alas, had not, being Superintendent of Spiritual Impediment has its drawbacks. Death is like the Post Office. Neither snow, nor rain, nor heat, nor one already successful intervention for the day, stays Death from the swift completion of his appointed rounds. My neck ached again after the affectionately applied Mick and Vick headlocks. My head throbbed dully, whether from the heat, the stress, or because I had chosen to ignore it for most of the day, I wasn't sure. Take your pick.

Clinique began to whimper in the back seat, and I turned to see what had induced this unusual behavior. She wasn't usually so subdued. She stared at the sunroof, or more accurately, she stared at the ghost who floated suspended near the sunroof, what with the more comfortable seating being taken up by two seven year olds, two backpacks, a soccer ball, and a suddenly nervous and whimpering Petit Basset Griffon Vendéen.

"No, no, no...please, not now," I murmured wearily, covering my face with my hands as if out of sight out of mind might have even a minute chance of working. Hadn't I just successfully rectified my first case? Doesn't a girl deserve a break?

"Clinique, stop whining," Denise reprimanded sharply. "Max, what's wrong?"

I thought full disclosure of the fact a ghost

currently hovered over her two heat-flushed and unsuspecting cherubs was probably not the best way to go. "My, uh head…yeah, my head is excruciatingly painful all of a sudden."

"You should have taken it easier today. But as usual, you don't listen to anybody. When we get back to the house, you should just go over to your place and lie down for a while. You probably overdid it," Denise admonished.

Well, that was easy. Go with the obvious, Max. And it wasn't even a lie. Within seconds, it had become a self-fulfilling prophesy.

Chapter Seven

By the time I dragged myself into the kitchen, the terrible twosome happily elected my father their jungle gym substitute, one hanging from each arm, and supplementing their chatter with whoops and squeals. The ever popular strains of Clinique howling compounded the racket.

My new translucent friend stuck to me like I was cadaver catnip. My stepmother looked better from a swelling perspective, though she still appeared pale and drawn to me. I wondered if I was the only one who noticed, or is this what Denise had been alluding to earlier?

Gail high-tailed it into the bathroom after one look at my festering arm, and returned with a bottle of calamine and a gourmet selection of antihistamines. While I slathered lotion and popped a couple of pills, Denise put the onion rings into the microwave and launched into a recap of our afternoon adventure.

I knew Gail would have a cake in the oven within the hour and a shopping bag packed with coffee, rolls, and paper products to take over to Adele's once the sad news broke. It was her standard bereavement offering.

I left them to it after reiterating my headache excuse, and retired to my apartment amid sympathetic murmurs and suggestions for relief, closely trailed by my new, transparent comrade who had yet to say a word—for which I was profoundly grateful. I wondered if he would continue to hover there by the sofa and remain silent if I continued to ignore him. I should have known better.

Suspended there in my living room, he looked like a golf pro wannabe in sharply pressed khakis and a casual yellow golf shirt. He was a stranger, and for that I was thankful. He told me his name was Ernesto and he was the driver of the car that had T-boned someone at an intersection just outside of town a few days ago. Seems he'd stopped for a beer after a round of golf and had one too many. His eyes were filled with ashes of memory, broken bones, and pain. He was sorry. I forgave him.

Unfortunately, it wasn't my forgiveness he needed. It turns out the woman in the other vehicle, who currently lay somewhere in a medically induced coma designed to minimize cerebral swelling, surrounded by a battery of blinking machines and an army of prayerful relatives, did not have health insurance. Don't even get me started on the current state of health care and insurance. Suffice it to say I strongly feel there is something inherently wrong with a system that allows a group of uninformed bureaucrats in suits with no medical knowledge to dictate what care may or may not be delivered in a situation better evaluated by licensed and educated physicians.

But again, I digress.

Ernie, it seemed had more than a little *dinero* in the bank. I got the distinct impression a good portion of it was obtained by nefarious means, but he got a bit defensive when I pressed too hard. It appeared he was a pretty bright guy, in fact, he was frankly glowing a little at the moment, but that isn't what I mean. He knew he couldn't undo what he'd done, but neither could he move on until he'd at least provided some form of restitution. I think he was a little worried about where he might be moving on *to* and figured he'd better hedge his bets. Enter the temporarily appointed Superintendent of Spiritual Interventions.

At his suggestion, I pulled my poor, neglected laptop out from under the sofa. I wondered if Ernie was the smartass who'd written "Clean Me" in the dust covering the lid. Caesar doesn't spell that well. The battery, of course, was dead.

Ernie stuck a finger in the AC port, and suddenly there was a flash of lightning, a rainbow appeared, and angels began to sing.

Actually, the screen came on and the OS booted, but I swear it was almost the same thing.

Under Ernie's direction, I hacked into his email and sent a letter to his lawyers, ostensibly from him, directing them to settle a monetary gift on the unfortunate coma patient.

He mentioned a figure. I raised a brow.

"What?" he sputtered defensively. "That's a lot of money."

"Yep, sure is. Then again maybe not so much when you consider medical bills, months of rehabilitation, possibly adaptive equipment or home modifications for any residual deficits, child care, lost wages..." I tapered off suggestively.

Ernie regarded me stubbornly. "Hey, I worked hard for that money. I don't even have to give her anything, you know."

"You're right, you don't."

It dawned on me I really was pretty lucky. Wait…when did I come to that conclusion? But, it was true. If it wasn't for my monthly alimony check and the support of my family, I could easily be the one in this poor woman's position. When was the last time I'd let myself acknowledge it? Sure, I resented it when Denise bought me things or offered to bail me out financially. I resented it because I felt like a poor relation having my nose rubbed in my failures. I'm the older sister, I should be taking care of her, right? Well, at any rate, Ernie could well afford to compensate his victim for his mistake. I punched in a few more zeros, and felt sure Ernie would have paled visibly if he wasn't already sporting a colorless, ghostly complexion.

"Are you crazy?" he demanded.

"Can't take it with you, Ernie," I countered, and he couldn't argue. He didn't look happy, but he waved me on and gave me the information on the woman, henceforth known as the unsuspecting millionaire, and I entered his instructions exactly as he dictated. Frankly, I didn't see how this could possibly work since Ernie had been dead for three days by his estimation, but when I checked his "sent" folder, sure enough the email I had just composed and dispatched logged as having been sent a week ago. Must be one of those nifty SSI superpowers Marv had so vaguely and unhelpfully referred to. Cool beans!

Before I could repeat the process and bestow a cool million on myself and a few close personal friends, Ernie removed his finger and the screen went black. And then, like Jeb Taber before him, Ernesto vanished. I wondered uneasily if my coercing him into increasing the dollar amount would reflect poorly on my keeping my end of the bargain. But, he was gone, so I hoped it was a good sign.

Thinking I might need the laptop again and worried the next ghost might not be as computer savvy as old Ernesto, I figured it might be a good idea to charge it.

On my hands and knees, I waved my arm around under the sofa for the power cord. One gym sock, two catnip mice, a family of dust bunnies, and a partridge in a pear tree later, my fingers closed around it. Using the questionably salvageable sock to swipe off the remaining dust, I plugged the cord in and left the computer on the kitchen counter to charge.

My cell phone beeped, and I dug it out of the bottom of my purse to find a text from Denise wondering if I was coming back over to Dad's for dinner, a la grill, of course.

I declined, surprised to find I actually felt conflicted and a bit disappointed, but I was still a little nauseated from the headache. I texted back she should send one of the rug rats over for the salad still hoping to get lucky beneath the plastic wrap in the fridge. Before long, I heard the pitter patter—yeah, let's go with that—of four little feet in soccer cleats pounding up my stairs. While I handed Mick the salad bowl, thankful that even without pre-planning I'd elected to use plastic, Vick made a beeline for Caesar. Poor guy never saw it coming. One wrestling match, mounds of flying fur, and a crying child later, Caesar had retired to the bedroom and the girls were on their way back to the grill-fest after I'd kissed the minor scratches on Vicki's arm with a promise it would make them all better.

Hey, kids believe that stuff.

When my cell rang a few minutes later, I knew it

was Denise calling to berate me for allowing one of her children to be attacked by a wild animal while in my care. But it wasn't Denise calling to give me a piece of her mind. It was worse. It was Roger. I let it go to voicemail and followed Caesar into the bedroom. I found the biggest, comfiest sleep shirt I owned, a soft pink number depicting a female mouse with her hair in curlers and holding a giant coffee mug, proclaiming "I don't do mornings". Roger bought it for me five years ago while at a seminar in Orlando. He said it reminded him of me. I don't know why. I never wear curlers.

I slathered some more calamine on my arm and then wrapped it with gauze to keep from scratching in my sleep. I pulled on a matching pair of pink fuzzy slipper socks and settled myself in bed against a pile of pillows, firmly clutching the TV remote, ready for action like the party girl I am.

My head truly pounded now, and I was sore and achy all over. But, hey, I'd managed to log two successful spiritual interventions today. I was on a roll. Yay, me! And with absolutely no help from Marvin Jenks, thank you very much.

The ibuprofen and heating pad weren't working and I had a passing thought maybe I should bring out the big guns: Beer and mentholated muscle cream. Then I decided the hangover wouldn't be worth it and the cream would leave me smelling like a one hundred and thirty pound breath mint. What I needed more than anything was sleep, lots and lots of sleep. I needed to curl up in my fifteen hundred count Egyptian cotton sheets, cocooned in my taupe velour blanket, and sleep like a well-fed baby.

Scratch that. Why do people always say they want

to sleep like a baby? Everyone knows babies never sleep.

No, I didn't want to sleep like a baby. I wanted to sleep like a ninety year old man in a hot church on Sunday.

I'd just managed to get comfortable when it happened. I tried to ignore the sensation, but resistance was futile. I thought of the desert. I pictured my feet, sadly in need of a pedicure. I thought of Texas in August. Heck, I pictured every dry and arid thing I could think of, without success. Some things in life are certain—the sun rises in the east, Santa Claus lives at the North Pole, and diuresis occurs when the body assumes a recumbent position. My kidneys are amazing. In fact, they pretty much operate autonomously, but they do need information from elsewhere in the body to tell them what to do. Things like changes in the composition of my body fluid, the stretch of my arterioles going into my glomeruli, and the fact I am lying down, incredibly comfortable, and almost asleep.

The major reason so many homebuyers insist on having a bathroom *en suite* has nothing to do with the luxury of Carrere Luxor Bath Towels, Italian marble, or Chastings Corque Corian Square Ceiling Mount Showerheads. It has nothing to do with resale value or having a separate spa-like retreat that is off limits to kiddies and houseguests. No, the real reason the average consumer is hell-bent on having a bathroom en suite is it significantly reduces the distance that must be traversed when the "I-am-lying-down-incredibly-comfortable-and-almost-asleep" receptors in the kidney are activated in the middle of the night and the urge to pee becomes overwhelming and unavoidable.

I was going to have no choice but to crawl out of my little cocoon of contentment and get up. The average capacity of the normal adult bladder may be sufficient to hold about a pint before distention sets in, discomfort ensues, and the alarm bells go off, but my bladder has the capacity of a lima bean.

Don't you hate it when you find exactly the right spot, are just about to doze off, and you have to pee? Happens to me every time.

Grumbling under my breath, I heeded nature's call and stumbled back to my bed. By the time the urge struck again and I opened my eyes, brilliant sunlight was spilling through the slats of the shuttered windows. Against all odds, I had enjoyed an entire night of undisturbed sleep. No phone calls from ex-husbands, no needy uninvited ghosts, no further calls of nature.

I know, right? I couldn't believe it either.

It was Sunday morning and given my recent death, I wondered if I should consider attending church with Dad and Gail. Then I reflected it would provoke far too much comment and decided against it.

The bowl of oatmeal and the raisin toast Gail had sent over yesterday was still in the casserole dish covered with foil on the kitchen counter, but regretfully I doubted it could be resuscitated at this point. I put a pot of coffee on to brew and popped a frozen bagel into the toaster oven. I was pretty sure I had exceeded the expiration date, but I preferred to think of those as suggestions, anyway. As a rule, I am something of a bagel snob. I prefer them thick and fresh and slathered in cream cheese and maybe a dollop of raspberry jam.

On Sunday mornings, I am also something of a

slug. Given the choice between lounging around in fuzzy slipper socks eating frozen bagels versus getting showered, dressed, and driving downtown for fresh bagels, frozen wins out every time. That's just how I roll.

While I waited for the timer, I tossed the ruined raisin toast in the trash and scraped the hardened and shriveled remains of the oatmeal out of the casserole dish. I left it to soak and then dumped a can of food into Caesar's blue ceramic dish and topped off his water.

He waddled out of the bedroom for a lick and sniff, but remained largely unimpressed. He scrambled up on the back of the couch and went back to sleep.

The toaster oven beeped and I buttered my bagel and poured a cup of coffee, ignoring the sizzle as it continued to drip onto the heating element since it was not quite finished brewing. Nothing says morning like the smell of burnt coffee. Someday I'm going to get one of those handy dandy coffeemakers that stop brewing when you take out the carafe to pour a cup. Or maybe I'll get one like Gail's and play musical coffee every morning.

I set everything on the island/breakfast bar and opened the door to get the paper. For once, the paperboy had managed to fling the rolled bundle near the top of the steps. His arm never made it all the way to the porch itself, and if it did, he ended up overcompensating and it sailed right over the top and out into the back yard. I snapped off the rubber band, dropped it in the end table drawer, and planted myself on the barstool. I moved the coffee and bagel to the side to allow plenty of room to spread out the paper.

My head felt pretty good this morning and my arm

was only mildly annoying. I gnawed determinedly at the rubbery bagel and then filled my mouth with enough coffee to turn it to mush so I could swallow it without the risk of aspiration. If only the raisin toast had still been edible. I tore off another bite of my bagel while browsing the front page of the paper. Just as I started turning the page, a small article caught my eye. It was squeezed in near the bottom, almost as an afterthought.

Local Woman Struck by Bus

The blurb went on to say a Hamilton woman had been struck about nine last night while waiting at a bus stop in Beaumont and had been taken to Beaumont South ER. There were no details, no name, no condition given, but I felt my stomach lurch anyway. Hamilton is a small town. I'm pretty sure I might have mentioned that?

Well, if I haven't, now you know.

The chances were good I knew this person, at least casually. I hoped the poor woman was okay.

Caesar began to hiss and spit and I turned to see what his problem was. That's when I knew the woman hit by the bus was not okay. I also knew her more than casually. Gerri Grubly, Bob the Front End Manager's wife, and the mother of four, sat on my couch. Her bright red hair was sprayed and teased to an unbelievable size. I hadn't seen hair so big since that Jersey rock band spent their summer Livin' on a Prayer.

I thought about Bob, overweight and disheveled, punching the time clock day after day to make ends meet, and the four Grubly kids whose mother would never come home. I didn't want to do this. Whatever Gerri's unfinished business, I *so* did not want to do this.

I wondered if there was a way to conjure up Marvin and call in sick for the day?

"Hey, Max," Gerri said sadly.

"Hey, Ger. Gosh, I don't even know what to say."

"I know, hard to believe, isn't it? One minute I was waiting for the bus, and the next minute I was under it. It happened so fast I never even saw it coming."

I could totally relate. The difference was, I'd been able to bargain my way back. Gerri was a nice girl, but not especially resourceful. I doubted she'd ever even heard of Kubler-Ross.

"Bob is at the hospital. They want him to pull the plug. I'm pretty sure I'm already gone, you know, but he can't accept it. You know Bob, Max, he's a good man, but he's a simple guy. He can't make that kind of a decision on his own." Her eyes filled with tears, whether for her own demise, Bob's dilemma, or both, I didn't know, and my throat felt too tight to ask.

"What about you parents, Gerri? Or his? Brothers, sisters?"

"My parents both passed years ago, and I haven't talked to my brother since Mom died. He wasn't real happy Bob and I got the house. Bob's folks moved out to Ohio not long after we graduated. They're on their way, but it's gonna take a while. Someone has to help him, Max."

"Me? You want *me* to go over to the hospital and tell Bob to pull the plug on you, Gerri? What makes you think he'll listen to me?" Oh God, I did not want to do this. I did not want to face Bob, wrinkled and distraught, weeping into his porn-stache at his wife's bedside, and then tell him he should pull the plug and go home to his four motherless kids.

"No, I couldn't ask you to do that, Max. I want you to give Bob a message for me. It'll help him know the right thing to do and then he'll be able to find peace with it eventually."

My throat felt tight and my chest ached. Part of me wanted to run into my Italian marble shower, smack my head off of the wall, go back to the poorly maintained bus station, and ask Marv to take me back and let Gerri go home to Bob and her kids. I thought maybe she was the better person. She had so much more to lose. But, somehow I didn't think it worked that way. I'd had unfinished business, but I didn't go anywhere near the SSI. I went straight to the OCP, because I wasn't supposed to die. But Gerri wasn't at the OCP, she was here with me. The situation didn't look promising.

"Oh God, Max, what'll happen to my kids? The older ones, they'll be okay, I think. But the little one…he won't even remember me in a few years. He won't remember what I was like, or what we did together, or how much I loved him. He won't understand I would never have left him if I had a choice." She sobbed quietly now, mascara streaming garishly down her ghostly cheeks.

"Sure he will, Gerri. You're his mother. Kids don't forget their mother." Do they? But how well did I remember mine? I'd been about the age of Gerri and Bob's youngest when I lost my mom. Oh, I remembered her in theory. I had photos, and I had some of her things. But, I didn't remember her favorite color or what it felt like to have her arms around me. I had no clear memory of her voice, or her smile, or her smell. I didn't know her as a person. When I remembered the voice that told me stories, the smile in the audience at my Christmas pageants, the arms that held me when I cried, the cool hand on my forehead when I was sick, none of them belonged to her. Did she cry too, when her time came, for the child who wouldn't know her? But, I'd been loyal, hadn't I? I hadn't let anyone horn in on her territory. No siree.

"Bob is a good man, Max, but he isn't strong enough to do this alone."

And I didn't know if I was strong enough to help him. I did not want to do this. But according to Gerri, there was no one else. If not me, who?

"Tell me what you need me to do."

****

Less than an hour later I stepped off of the elevator on the fifth floor at Beaumont South. The elevators were old and the doors groaned in weary protest as I impatiently pushed them aside and strode briskly to the nurses' station. Visiting hours were restricted to family only on this floor, and even then in limited increments.

Bob would be with Gerri, though. In her case it was a death watch, and they would have let him stay. The woman behind the desk had a huge mass of stiffly sprayed hair, in the most unnatural shade of red I'd ever seen. I wondered if she'd been one of Gerri's clients. She was a unit clerk and not any of the nurses I knew. I'd been hoping I would be able to convince one of them to let me in. Guess I'd have to play the Roger card.

"Hi," I smiled. "I'm Maxine McCoy, Dr. McCoy's wife? Can you please tell me what room Geraldine Grubly is in?"

"Dr. McCoy's ex-wife, you mean," she replied cattily. "I've heard about you."

Again I refer you to Small Town Rule Number One: if you don't remember your business, just ask the neighbors.

"Of course," I replied tightly, keeping the smile plastered on my face. "That's what I meant. Old habits die hard. So, Geraldine Grubly's room?"

"Mrs. McCoy," she explained patiently, as if to a small child. I tuned her out for a moment and concentrated on the fact I'd forgotten what it was like to be called Mrs. McCoy. "You know only immediate family is allowed in. How did you even know about Mrs. Grubly? The police haven't released the name yet."

"Why, uh, the family called me, of course. They're coming from out of town, but can't get here for hours. Since I am such a close personal friend, they asked if I could stop by and sit with Bob until they arrive."

"Oh," she said, looking less hostile and more uncertain. "Well, you know I'm not supposed to let you in, but the poor guy has been in there for hours all alone, and I guess it wouldn't hurt if you went in for a few minutes since you are such a good friend. Lord knows the man can use a friend right now. Maybe you can talk to him. The Organ Procurement Team is here. She carried a donor card, but he won't even speak to them. Such a tragedy...I heard they have a couple of kids."

"Yeah," I croaked sadly over the lump in my throat. "They do. Four of them."

The walk to room five fifty-two, seemed endless, one of the longest I could remember. The dim gray hallway was eerily silent, punctuated only by the brisk slap of my old tennis shoes echoing back from the countless doors of identical anonymity, and the faint beep, beep, beep of mechanical monitors reckoning the remaining moments of lives coming to an end. When I finally reached the room, the blinds were closed on both the door and the big glass observation window. I knocked softly and took a very deep breath before pushing the door slowly open.

Bob huddled in a chair at the side of the bed, his forehead resting on hands clutching the cold, still fingers of his wife. The only sound was the mechanical click-swoosh of the ventilator as it forced humidified air into lungs that no longer required it, and Bob's quiet sobs. He raised his head when I entered, and though I've known him for most of my life, I barely recognized him.

His face was soft and wrinkled like a used tissue, and tears saturated his porn-stache, leaving it corded and wiry like rat tails. He looked through me for a minute, like I was someone he'd never seen before, then something seemed to click and with a low moan, he reached toward me and began to sob, deep gut-wrenching sobs that choked him and left him gasping for breath.

I hurried to his side and he wrapped his arms around my waist, buried his face in my stomach, and shook with grief. I practiced what I would say all the way to the hospital, but now, faced with such overwhelming anguish, words failed me. What could I possibly say to this man? There were no smart-ass remarks, sarcastic comments, or acerbic observations to lighten the mood or distract attention away from the pain. That was what I did best. I'd mastered the art of avoidance. This was an agony that couldn't be diverted.

I remained silent, partly because I thought anything I could say was completely inadequate, and partly because my throat and chest felt so tight and congested I wasn't sure I could get a word out. I'm not much of a crier, myself, at least not in public where anyone can see me.

Away from prying eyes, that was a different story. I don't know why, but crying in front of people had always made me feel uncomfortable and vulnerable. I guess I was the strong, stoic type. Or at least that's what I told myself.

I waited, stroking Bob's head until, at last, he seemed to regain some composure. He sat back and swiped at his eyes, and I dug in my purse and came up with a rumpled tissue for each of us. Then I got the only other chair in the room and pulled it up beside his.

"They said Gerri is brain dead," he whispered brokenly. "They said she'll never wake up. They want me to pull the plug, Max. How do I do that? How do I give up on her? She's the only girl I ever loved. I don't know how to be in this world without her."

"I know," I finally choked out. "Bob, did you and Gerri ever talk about what she wanted if this ever happened?"

"What?" Bob regarded me blankly. "How could we ever think this would happen?"

"I mean if either one of you ever ended up in a condition like this."

Bob stood and began agitatedly pacing the confines of the small space like a caged animal desperate for a way out.

"We, uh…well, we talked about what we wanted if it was hopeless, but it isn't hopeless, right? They told me she's brain dead, but she could still come out of this." His voice cracked. He pointed at the cardiac monitor tracing regular green lines and maintaining a soft, steady beep. "See? Her heart is still beating. Touch her, Max, she's still warm. Dead people are cold, they're cold. How can she be dead if her heart's still beating and she's not even cold?"

Even if I hadn't had my little visit with Gerri earlier, I knew brain death was brain death, and it wasn't declared lightly or arbitrarily. Only after conducting a series of tests would the doctors have confirmed Gerri was brain dead, truly, irrevocably brain dead.

I tried to comprehend how traumatic it must be for anyone, let alone someone with Bob's limited understanding of anatomy and physiology. To him, his wife appeared to be alive, therefore she couldn't be dead. But, appearances were deceiving, and the appearance of life didn't make death any easier to accept. In fact, maybe it only made it harder.

"Bob, I wish I had an easy way to say this." I didn't. False hope was still hope and it's never easy to take that away. I didn't want to be the one to take it away. I wanted to tell him everything would be all right, but it wouldn't and that wasn't why I'd been sent. Even if I knew less about medicine than I did, even if I wanted to ignore all I knew to be true and still have hope, too, I knew Gerri was gone. I'd heard it right from her Passion's Promise painted lips.

"Bob, Gerri was probably gone before she ever got to the hospital. Her injuries were just not survivable, honey. She's warm because her heart is still beating. Her heart is still beating because of the medicines and the machines. Her body is here, Bob, but her personality, her mind, her spirit…everything that made her Gerri, is gone. They put her on mechanical support to keep her organs viable. There was a donor card in her wallet. Otherwise, they would have let her go. I'm so, so, sorry, Bob."

My voice cracked despite my best attempt. I really was sorry. Sorry I'd always kind of thought of Bob and Gerri as two geeky kids who got pregnant and then grew into two geeky adults dragging up four kids on minimum wage. Sorry I hadn't thought very much of them, if I ever bothered to think about them at all. No matter what my opinion had been, they had shared something special and loving and forever. Why had I ever thought I had any right to judge?

"She always helped people," Bob said woodenly. "We didn't have much, but my Gerri would give a person the shirt off her back. She was just like that, you know? Look at how she went back to beauty school. It wasn't easy with money so tight and four kids to worry about and me working full time, but she set her mind to it and she did it. She only wanted to make people feel better about themselves."

"And isn't that a wonderful thing to tell your children, a wonderful way to remember her?" I took a deep breath and swallowed hard. "Look at her, Bob. Think about the Gerri you know. What do you think she'd tell you right now if she could?"

He stared at the bed, silent tears streaming down his face. He looked like a big, wet walrus. Under the circumstances, I wish I could come up with a more flattering analogy, but it is what it is. Gerri lay pale and still, her trademark red hair completely hidden under the layers of stark, white bandages covering her head, her now nude lips stretched and contorted by the endotracheal tube taped to her mouth and passed down her throat. Her chest rose and fell in the rhythm of the ventilator. Bags of IV fluids and medications hung from metal poles all around the bed, stimulating the heart to continue beating.

I was about to tell him what she would say, because she'd asked me to. It didn't make it any easier to know the message I would give him came right from Gerri, herself. I still felt like I was coercing him into doing something he wasn't ready to face. He dropped his face into his hands and his broad shoulders shook. Then he raised his eyes to mine, and I hope I never see such a look of naked grief on anyone's face again.

"She didn't ever want this. I promised her I wouldn't ever let this happen. I know what I have to do Max, I just don't know how to do it. How do you let go of your best friend?"

I didn't have the easy answer to that. I wasn't sure I had ever successfully let go of my own, and I hadn't been faced with a decision nearly as final as this.

"You don't, Bob. You don't ever let her go. She'll always be a part of you and a part of your kids. And it's up to you to keep her memory alive for them, especially little Robbie. She'd like that. And I know it doesn't feel like it now, but someday, if someone comes along that helps to heal your heart and makes you happy, then you grab it with both hands, because if there's one thing I know, it's that Gerri loved you and would want you to be happy. She, uh, told me that once."

I wrapped my arms around Bob's big shoulders and held him while he cried. He might not be the brightest bulb in the chandelier, but Bob Grubly knew how to love with his whole heart. His wife had been a lucky woman. I would never in a million years have chosen to be here. But, I guess, in a way, I did choose it when I entered into the bargain with Marvin to become the temporary SSI.

I hadn't given it much thought, it had served my purpose at the time. I didn't expect any part of it would hurt so much. In ways I'd never expected. I didn't own an umbrella big enough for this shit storm I found myself in.

At Bob's request, I stayed with him and Gerri while the Organ Procurement Team came in and spoke with him. They were as kind and compassionate as they could be under the circumstances, and kept emphasizing the incredible gift Gerri was giving and the lives she would change. Bob was somber and polite, and I'm not sure he actually processed a word they said. But everyone agreed they could wait until Bob's parents and sister arrived from Ohio before proceeding with the harvesting. They arrived within the hour and after expressing my condolences, I excused myself.

"Max?" Bob called after me as the door eased shut. I stopped and stuck my head back in. "I just want to say thanks. I don't know what made you come, but thanks for sitting with Gerri and for talking to me. Thanks for being a friend when I needed one. I wasn't strong enough to do this on my own."

"Sometimes you never know how strong you are, Bob, until strong is the only choice you have."

"Well, having a hand to hold doesn't hurt. Thank you."

I waved as I slipped out and let the door close

behind me, because I wasn't sure I could get another word out. The not crying thing? Yeah, well, I was about to lose it in a major way, and I didn't think it would help Bob or his family to witness my meltdown.

I hurried back past the desk, happy to see the unit clerk was busy on the phone so she wouldn't try to engage me in conversation. The elevator was opening as I approached and as soon as the housekeeper pushed her cart clear, I jumped in and hit the button before anyone could join me.

The elevator doors ground open in the lobby and I closed my eyes in relief. I was almost out of the hospital and I hadn't run into a single person I knew. Once I was safely locked in my car, I could let it all out. I was going to make it! Across the lobby I could see the revolving door glinting in the sun, whirling, teasing, beckoning, beckoning…I was almost there…

I should have known when something seems too good to be true, it generally is.

Chapter Eight

"Max? What are you doing here? Is everything all right?"

Eight more steps and everything would have been fine. I would have been out the door. I so could not deal with Roger right now. I stopped as he hurried across the lobby to where I stood.

"Is it your head?"

"Hello, Roger." I said as I turned "My head's fine, thanks."

He glanced down at the gauze adorning my arm "What did you do to your arm?"

"Poison oak. It's fine."

His brows went up to his hairline, disappearing beneath the wayward lock that always seemed to tumble down over his forehead. I used to find it charming. Okay, I still found it charming. Hey, I never said Roger was not an attractive guy. Dark hair, dark eyes, great smile. Dressed in dark slacks and a snug gray tee topped with a casual black sport jacket as he was now, he was...well he was sex in a suit. Not that I noticed.

Nope, not at all. That's my story and I'm sticking to it.

I'd left the house this morning having given little thought to my appearance. The occasion hadn't seemed to warrant a push up bra and low rise jeans. Sweat pants, tennis shoes, and a layered tank didn't exactly compliment Roger's sleek GQ look, but hey, I wasn't trying to impress anyone, anyway, least of all my ex-husband. Right? At least my dark, unruly hair brushed my shoulders in thick, soft waves today instead of a nest of questionable dreadlocks, thanks to Denise's follicular intervention. Okay, maybe it would have been nice to look especially hot and hope he lamented what he was missing. Hindsight is twenty-twenty, they say.

Yeah, I'd pretty much adopted the phrase as my mantra.

"Poison oak? Where the heck did you get that?" His surprise was understandable. Roger was well-acquainted with my lack of enthusiasm for outdoor life.

"Long story." He squinted down at me. I knew the last hour or so must be showing on my face. Roger knew me better than anyone. At least I thought he did. Apparently he didn't know me well enough to realize I didn't share well with others. Go figure.

"I stopped in to check on a patient. I didn't expect to run into you here. What's wrong?"

"Yeah, well that makes two of us. I didn't expect to run in to you, either. Everything is peachy keen, Rog…gotta run. Buh-bye."

He grabbed my arm when I would have turned back toward the door. The poison oak-less one, I couldn't help noticing. "Max, you're lying."

"Unlike you, Roger, I don't lie. I prefer to think of it as strategically misinforming."

"You know what? I don't know why I bother. You haven't had a civil word to say to me in over a year. We were married for thirteen freaking years. I guess maybe I can't turn it off as easily as you can. I worry about you. So, sue me." He forked a hand through his hair in frustration.

"You worry about me? That's rich, Roger. Were you worried about me while you were gazing into Boobie's eyes over the truffle pasta?"

"We are *not* going to do this in the lobby. C'mon." He dragged me back the way I'd come, past the elevators, and opened the door to an empty on-call room near the ER. I fought the urge to dig my heels in, whine and wail, and make him physically drag me, but people were already beginning to stare and the last time I'd made that kind of a scene, I'd lost my Spaghetti alla Carbonara privileges. Sure, I could get it at the Pasta Hut, but it wasn't the same. They poured a jar of Alfredo sauce on over-cooked noodles, crumbled bacon on top, and called it Carbonara. Heathens.

Roger pulled me inside and closed the door, standing in front of it so I would have to physically move him to get out. "Now," he demanded, breathing heavily. "What's wrong?"

"Nothing's wrong…it's just been a totally, incredibly bad morning. Now if you don't mind, I have to go."

"Well, I do mind," he returned hotly. "I'm going to talk, and you're going to listen. Did you get my message?"

"No, I didn't check my phone this morning…something, um, came up."

"Fine, well I need you to stop by the office tomorrow afternoon and sign some papers."

"I already signed the only papers that matter, Roger, and you are not cutting my alimony. We've been through this," I said stubbornly.

"Oh for God's sake, Max, give it a rest. You'll get your damn alimony. I'm going out of the country for a while, and I want to give you my durable power of attorney."

"Why?" Then his words registered. "Why do you need to give anyone a POA?" Obviously the OCP acronym thing was contagious. Marv could have warned me I might be prone to speaking in initials. At least I would have been prepared.

"I'm going to Somalia. You knew I was planning this before the divorce. You wouldn't listen then, and you haven't listened since. I met with Barb that night to discuss my qualifications. She's the liaison for Humanitarian Partnership."

"Well, lucky you, she apparently found you more than qualified. Please, Roger, how naïve do you think I am? I may be young but I wasn't born yesterday! I know what I saw."

"No, Max, you decided what you thought you saw. Do you honestly think I would be stupid enough to take another woman to a place where everyone knows the both of us if I was having an affair?"

"Sure, if you were hoping someone else would tell me and save you the trouble."

"Oh my God, you can rationalize anything to keep from admitting you might have been wrong, can't you? You have everything all figured out and tied up with an ugly little bow. It must be nice to be so incredibly sure of yourself all the time. You made up your mind in an instant and you never looked back."

He couldn't be more wrong. I looked back all the time. Shows how much he knows!

"Oh really? And I guess you and she have been

discussing business for the last year and a half, too?"

"Is that your subtle way of asking if I've slept with her? Yes, I have. Do you feel vindicated now, Max? Well, don't give yourself too much credit. It was brief, it was mutually casual, and it was *never* while I was still with you. You know what? I don't even know why I'm explaining this yet again. We've been over and over this and nothing changes. You believe what you want to believe, regardless of the truth."

"I have to leave now."

"Just come and sign the papers, Max." He sighed tiredly. "Hey, at least you'll be assured of getting your alimony checks, right? That should make you happy. The bottom line is I need to know if something happens, my affairs will be taken care of by someone I can trust. And while I don't like you very much sometimes, I do trust you. And isn't that ironic considering your complete lack of faith in me?"

He didn't like me? What's not to like?

"Geez, Roger, you sure know how to charm a girl. If I agree to sign your damn papers, will you just let me leave?"

Because if I didn't get out of here soon, I was going to cry. In front of him. It was because of the whole scene with Bob, of course. I'm not much of a crier, remember? Not in public, and most especially not in a deserted on-call room with my ex-husband. I didn't want Roger thinking it had anything to do with him. It didn't, of course. I knew he'd been sleeping with Barbara. I just didn't expect it to hurt so much to hear him actually say it. Whoever said the truth hurts was right. Boy, were they right! But I guess it's better to be told a hurtful truth than a comforting lie. I thought of

Jeb Taber. He'd said everyone needs to feel needed. I hadn't let Roger feel needed even at a time when I'd needed him the most. I hadn't let anyone feel needed, not in a long time. Because I didn't want to need anyone.

"So you'll stop in tomorrow? Make it sometime after noon, okay? I'll be in the OR until at least eleven." He stepped away from the door and I pulled it open.

"What about your patients? When you go to Somalia, I mean?"

"I'm referring them to Kramer until I get back."

"Kramer? Oh Lord, Roger! I thought you cared about your patients. He's a total hack."

"He's not a hack, he's completely competent. Oh, but I guess I should remember your low opinion of proctologists as a whole," he said, and I detected a hint of bitterness in his tone.

"What are you talking about? My low opinion of you has nothing to do with your profession and everything to do with your infidelity. Sometimes you are such an ass, Roger."

"And there it is! Can't pass up an opportunity to get in a dig, can you? Enough with the ass cracks, already," he said angrily. Then he realized what he said—I could tell by the look on his face.

Remarkably, I let it pass.

I know, it surprised me, too.

He thought I had a low opinion of him because he was a proctologist? I thought about all of the times I'd commented on the fact he could have been anything, a neurosurgeon, a researcher, a transplant specialist. I'd never understood why he'd chosen proctology, but that didn't mean I didn't think he was the best damn proctologist there was. I thought I was being supportive, I thought he was brilliant.

When no sarcastic remark was forthcoming, he grinned ruefully. "Well, I guess I walked right into that one, huh?"

I bit my lip and couldn't help grinning back. "Yeah, you kinda did."

Our eyes met and, I admit, I was the first to look away. I wasn't a coward, mind you, it was only that I'd already had all of the emotionally draining drama I could handle in the space of a few short hours.

I took a deep breath. I figured I'd better spit it out before my bitch gene kicked back in. "Roger, I never understood why you chose the specialty you did, but I never thought less of you for it. You would excel at anything."

I didn't mean for it to sound like I was having teeth pulled. It was difficult to offer him a compliment, but it wasn't fair to let him think I'd been ashamed of what he did, or I hadn't supported him. I wondered if it had been my attitude that had caused him to feel that way. Oh, wait, that's right, I don't have an attitude. Must have been him. That's my story and I'm sticking to it.

He looked surprised, then shyly pleased. "I guess we never really talked about it, did we? You know why I chose proctology? Diseases of the colon, the rectum, and the anus? Working with urologists, and gynecologist to deal with interrelated issues when they occur? Can you think of any other areas of the body that are more embarrassing or difficult for patients to discuss or seek treatment for? They need to feel like they can discuss these things openly and honestly with their doctor. That's the doctor I try to be. How many surgeons do you know who are so focused on the procedure they lose sight of the patient's fears and concerns in the shuffle? It may not be the most glamorous specialty, but I didn't become a doctor to win awards or become wealthy. I do this because I want to heal people and improve their quality of life. And I think I do. At least I hope I do. I'm sorry if it wasn't the lifestyle you expected." His voice vibrated with passion. He'd always been passionate about the things that were important. It was the Roger I'd fallen in love with.

"You have no idea what my expectations were, Roger." I sighed wearily. "And at the risk of sounding redundant, I *really* can't do this today. I promise I'll stop by tomorrow if that will put an end to this little tete-a-tete, okay?"

"Fair enough."

That was my cue to make my escape. But, something still bothered me. "You think Kramer will give your patients the same compassion and attention?" I frowned.

"I'll only be gone a month." He laughed. "Kramer will manage."

Of course, he would. I wasn't as sure about the patients, though. Oh, Kramer was competent, as Roger said, but he truly *was* an ass, and I mean that in ways which have nothing to do with proctology.

He won't touch a case if it has a chance of anything but a positive outcome. His perfect track record is far more important to him than any patient. All that aside, he was a total sleaze-ball. I hoped none of Roger's referrals would need anything more than routine colonoscopies or a prescription for hemorrhoid cream while he was away. Oh, well, not my problem. My colon was just fine, thanks.

"Yeah, you're right, I'm sure he'll manage. I'll see you tomorrow," I turned to go. He reached out and put a hand on my bare shoulder. Okay, so maybe I shivered a little, but it was probably the air conditioning. I swear.

"Hey, let me give you a script for something for the poison oak," he offered, hesitantly removing his hand so slowly it almost felt like a caress. He reached into his jacket for a prescription pad. "It must be pretty itchy."

"Thanks, but I'm fine."

"So, what *were* you doing here?"

"Visiting a friend." And the recollection of that suddenly put all of my bitchy gripes and petty problems into perspective.

"I'll see you tomorrow," he called after me, but I didn't bother to turn and acknowledge it. I was pretty sure Roger and I would live to fight another day. It was more than I could say for Gerri and Bob Grubly.

****

Denise's SUV was already hunkered down in the drive grinning at me, and Dad and Gail were just getting home from church and climbing out of their car as I barreled into the drive. I jammed the gearshift into park and left the windows open in case I had occasion to go out again today. I didn't plan on it, but my plans seemed to have had very little bearing on my actual activities over the last few days.

Gail used sign language and temptingly waved a bag of fresh bagels and Long Johns in the air to indicate I should come over. I had to hand it to her, she was persistent. The Logan family Sunday morning post-church coffee klatch was a scheduled event that never varied. Attendance was considered mandatory, but I usually managed to time my arrival right as things were breaking up, which limited my exposure to the one-big-happy-family vibe. I waved back and headed for my stairs out of habit. Then I remembered a condescending cat and some frozen bagels were the only things awaiting me at my place. Maybe just this once I should refrain from biting the hand bearing the coffee.

If anyone felt compelled to comment on the fact I had elected to join in the jocularity unusually early, they managed to remain remarkably reticent, for which I was grateful. Well, the adults, at any rate. Mick and Vick were less subdued, tugging at me in tandem, each more persistent than the other, babbling non-stop in competition to be heard, and Clinique lapped me in happily howling circles. Gail plopped a plate of Long Johns in the middle of the table and went back to slicing bagels while Denise took orders for coffee and poured the Half and Half into a little pottery creamer that looked like a rooster. I initially made a move to help, and then realized they'd long ago worked out a system which didn't include me.

Brad-the-Famous-Vascular-Surgeon and his black socked, sandal clad feet had retreated to the family room to set up the TV trays for the twins. Clinique, relatively quiet at last, abandoned me in favor of her lord and master. Gail noticed me standing awkwardly to the side and spun around with two paper plates bearing identically toasted bagels heavy on the cream cheese.

"Here, Max," she said. "Give these to Frick and Frack. It's the only way to get a moment of silence. And there's a steak bone wrapped in foil in the fridge for Clinique, if you wouldn't mind. Put it on the tile over by the fireplace so she doesn't slop it all over the carpet."

Finally feeling useful, I did as she asked, and at last, the terrible twosome quietly chomped away, their gums glued together with cream cheese and their attention captured by cartoons. Clinique devoted her attention to the Grill Master's leftovers, and all was right with the world, at least for the ten seconds it took me to pull up a chair and gratefully accept a mug of espresso from Denise and a Long John from my father.

Brad-the-Famous-Vascular-Surgeon's beeper chose that moment to go off, and I saw his eyes go to Denise's and hers glimmer with moisture. He excused himself to use the phone in my father's office. Denise rose and turned her back to the table to stare out the window over the sink, and I saw her knuckles were white where she gripped the counter.

"Honey, what is it?" Gail asked, beating me to the punch.

Denise hesitated a moment, then took a deep breath and turned around. She swiped at her eyes and then sighed. "Gerri Grubly was hit by a bus and killed last night. They were keeping her on life support because she was an organ donor. Bob was really struggling and Brad asked Diane, the clerk on five, to beep him when there was any news," Denise said quietly.

"Oh, my, gosh, that's awful," Gail exclaimed, and Dad shook his head in disbelief.

"Yeah, it is," Denise agreed. "Their Kirsten played on the twin's soccer team last year. Brad and Bob coached together. Such nice people. Those poor kids."

Brad re-entered the room, and at Denise's look, shook his head sadly. "It's over. Diane said that at least

Bob's folks were there with him at the end." He turned to regard me with an odd expression on his face. "She also said you'd been there earlier and sat with Bob for quite a while. She said you were the one who convinced Bob to talk to the Organ Procurement people. I told her she must have you confused with someone else."

Four sets of eyes swiveled toward me. It was hard to say which set looked more surprised.

"Um, yeah…I stopped by earlier and kept Bob company until his folks got there. What?" I asked defensively, tearing off a mouthful of doughnut. I had no idea if I could swallow it over the lump lodged firmly in the vicinity of my chest, but it gave me something to concentrate on besides the fact my entire family stared at me like I'd grown another head.

Can you spell low expectations, boys and girls?

"Nothing, I just would never have expected…I mean, um…I didn't know you knew Bob all that well," Denise finished lamely.

But, I knew what she really meant. I hadn't exactly been in the habit of putting myself out for anyone lately. "They were talking about it at the SuperSave this morning," I said, lying as smoothly as butter on hotcakes. I hadn't been anywhere near the SuperSave this morning, but none of them knew that. "Someone mentioned Bob's folks were coming in from out of town, but wouldn't be there for a while. I figured I wouldn't want to be alone under the circumstances, so I stopped by to see if there was anything I could do. No big deal."

I didn't feel the need to share the fact that I hadn't had a choice. Would I have gone on my own if I really had heard the news through the grapevine at the

SuperSave? Not a snowball's chance in hell. I was ashamed to realize it would never even have occurred to me. Could I honestly say I was sorry I had been there? As difficult as it had been for me, I knew it couldn't even begin to approach how difficult it had been, and would continue to be, for Bob and his family. If my being there helped in some small way? Well, I guess I couldn't be sorry about that, could I?

"That was incredibly...thoughtful of you," Gail said, failing miserably to conceal her shock.

I shrugged. Well, hell, they didn't have to all act as though my being thoughtful was a sign of the impending Apocalypse. I think I should be offended.

I smiled at Gail and couldn't help thinking she seemed a bit off. Denise had mentioned yesterday that she was concerned, too. She thought something might be bothering her Mom, and I wondered if it might be more than that. Her color even seemed a bit gray, but maybe it was the lighting.

She excused herself to go to the bathroom, and when she returned she looked even paler. She also looked like she could use a nap even though it was barely noon. I looked around. No one else seemed to notice anything was amiss. Maybe I was overreacting to the events of the day.

Gail seemed to become aware I was watching her closely and offered a bright, encouraging smile. I didn't know whether she intended to commend me for my actions at the hospital, or to indicate she'd noticed my concerned interest and wanted to reassure me everything was fine. Either way, it seemed a bit forced.

I looked away, and then got up to help Denise, who had started to clear the table. Dad and Brad made their way out to the back yard to discuss the benefits of lawn aeration versus dethatching, and the twins, Mick with a soccer ball and Vick bravely clasping Clinique's leash, weren't far behind. I vaguely noted this was the point at which I usually arrived and wolfed down a bagel and coffee before making a hasty exit. Today I'd survived the entire coffee klatch, and to my surprise, it hadn't been the least bit painful.

After loading the dishwasher and waving off Denise and company who were headed for an afternoon soccer game, I headed to my place to check on Caesar. While Dad puttered in the shed, Gail started a list of the items for her bereavement package for the Grubly family. I somehow knew in addition to her standard fare, she would be adding in something special for those kids.

The rest of the day passed uneventfully enough, interrupted only by the roar of my father and his lawn tractor passing under my windows periodically. I thought maybe Death or Marvin, or both, had thoughtfully decided to cut me a break for the remainder of the day by taking only those who'd managed to wrap up all of their loose ends in advance.

By the time I donned my mouse in curlers tee and crawled into my fifteen-hundred count Egyptian cotton for the night, I managed to catch up on all of my laundry, write out all of the bills, vacuum the area rugs, and scoot the dust-mop over the hardwood. Remembering the warren of dust bunnies I'd disturbed following Ernesto's visit, I even remembered to clean under the sofa after sobbing my way through a movie on the classic movie channel.

Caesar observed it all curiously, wearing a faintly

disturbed expression. I think he feared I might be a Doppelganger.

Chapter Nine

Monday morning, I showered early and dressed with care. Since my last two run-ins with Roger had caught me at a distinct disadvantage and shown me in a less than flattering light, fashion-wise I mean, I planned to look my best. Fortunately, it wasn't too difficult to outclass hospital gowns and sweatpants.

I examined myself in the mirror with a critical eye. I imagined the slim, black slacks and strappy, high heeled sandals made my legs look longer, while the powder blue silk V-neck shell made my blue eyes pop and clung flirtatiously to my water-bra assisted cleavage. Not that there was a brassiere made that would enable my modest girls to compete with Thing One and Thing Two, but one makes do with what one has.

My dark hair fell around my shoulders in thick waves, pulled back from my face in a faux sapphire encrusted clip holding a fall of hair I'd managed to artfully arrange in the back to camouflage most of my stapled gash. I applied a hint of blush, a touch of mascara, and some sheer tinted gloss in lieu of lipstick. I couldn't do much about the rash on my arm, but at least it had faded to pale pink and the blisters had dried and were no longer oozing. I dabbed a light coat of foundation over the discolored area with a make-up sponge and set it with powder. It wasn't perfect, but it would have to do. Of course, I didn't give a flying fig what Roger thought. I just didn't want the office staff to think I'd gotten a divorce and then let myself go.

That's my story and I'm sticking to it.

By the time I finished primping, the clock had barely moved past ten. I still had more than two hours before I was due at Roger's office and I wondered if I could manage to keep from spoiling my prettiness for that length of time. Fortuitously, or not, I had a visitor to distract me. I knew I had company when Caesar began to mewl piteously and tried to force his massive bulk behind the refrigerator—as if.

Myra appeared in a long sleeved flannel nightgown buttoned up to her wrinkled throat. Yes, it was still the middle of June. I guess the stereotypical assumption that old people are always cold is true. Her long, gray hair hung in a thick plait down the middle of her back, and I had to push Caesar from the arm of the couch when he kept trying to swat it. Sometimes my cat simply has no sense of propriety.

Myra was ninety-two years old and was currently growing cold and stiff in her bed in a charming craftsman style home on the south side of Beaumont. Coincidentally, her home was only about four blocks from the hospital and the adjacent medical arts building where Roger had his office. A pit stop was not out of the question should it be required. I would have thought ninety-two years would have been plenty long enough to take care of any unfinished business a body might have, but surprisingly, I was wrong.

I know, being wrong shocks me every time, too. But, hey, no one's perfect.

Myra had two granddaughters. The first one,

Susan, was a grandmother's dream and would, no doubt, be the unfortunate one to find the body later in the day when she arrived for her daily visit with a freshly arranged bouquet and a hot dinner complete with homemade desert. Susan took care of all of the grocery shopping, housekeeping, finances, medication management, and doctor's appointments. She was sweet, attentive, and loving, the veritable perfect example of a granddaughter.

The other girl, Corrine, not so much. It seems Corrine's proclivity for fast living, fast money, and fast, manipulative men had left the family broken and estranged.

Myra had made a will a few years ago barely acknowledging Corrine. Now in hindsight, which apparently becomes remarkably clearer on the other side of the cosmic divide, she felt compelled to give Corrine a second chance. Okay, so maybe this was Corrine's tenth or eleventh second chance, but Myra felt strongly you don't give up on those you love. Myra, it seemed, wished to dictate a codicil.

See, I knew plugging in that laptop was going to be a smart move.

For those of you as legalese challenged as I, it appears a codicil is a written amendment to a person's will that can add to, subtract from, or modify the terms of the original, and must make some reference to the will it is intended to amend. So far, so good. Myra talks and I type. That isn't so hard, but of course as usual, there is a sticking point. A codicil must also be dated, signed, and witnessed exactly as a will would be. So, how was that going to work?

I dated the document for two weeks earlier, easy

enough, loaded a sheet of paper into my printer, plugged the cable into the laptop, crossed my eyes, and hoped for the best. The printout that emerged was a beautiful thing, an early Christmas miracle that brought a tear to my eye. It came complete with a Notary seal and the witness signatures of Marvin Jenks and one Morgan Kane, whoever he was.

"Grim Reaper," Myra informed me with a knowing nod.

The only signature missing was Myra's, and she wasn't exactly in any state to hold a pen. At her urging, I signed her name in her stead and was astonished to see the resultant signature bore no similarity to my own and was obviously that of a feeble, elderly woman. Myra pronounced it perfect. Add an uncanny talent for forgery to the short list of SSI superpowers I had experienced thus far. I briefly wondered how soon Marv and company would catch up to me should I decide to use said superpowers for nefarious means. Just a hunch, but I doubted that fell under my keeping up my end of the bargain.

I expected Myra would want me to sneak the document into her little craftsman bungalow somehow, but she advised me instead to address an envelope to her lawyers and drop it in the mail. I had no doubt it would arrive at the legal offices with a postmark several days old. I didn't even question it. I guess I was catching on. Myra dissipated into eternity after advising me that I looked a little thin and should eat more. I knew I could probably stand to lose ten pounds, but I guess grandmothers are grandmothers, and apparently even the dead ones can't help themselves.

I left a little early so I would have time to swing by

the post office and take care of Myra's business. I suspected old faithful Susan wouldn't be too happy when the codicil came to light, but I secretly hoped Myra's plan worked, and Corrine straightened herself out and found her way back to her family and a decent life. Everyone deserves to have someone who never gives up on them.

Shortly before one, I pulled into the parking lot of the medical arts building connected by a walkway to Beaumont South Hospital. Luckily, some of the building's occupants were still out having a long lunch, so I slid into a parking spot a short distance from the main entrance. Back when I was Roger's Office Manager, I'd usually hitched a ride to work with him, unless he had early surgery that day, so I never had to worry about parking. The docs rate a reserved space. The doc's ex-wives, however, not so much.

Right inside the doors, Big Jim, the security guard sat parked behind his desk, eyes glued to the flickering black and white screens monitoring the different areas of the building via security cameras.

Predictable as ever, I could almost believe he hadn't moved since I'd last worked here. Gruff and grizzled, Jim's uniform shirts were always crisply pressed and his tie always hung straight as an arrow. He might not be a real policeman, but he sure took pride in looking the part.

His face lit up when he saw me striding through the doors, and he managed to tear his intent gaze away from the screens long enough to flash me a pleased, gleaming white smile that contrasted sharply with his dark skin.

Ah, it's good to be missed.

"Hey, little girl! How've you been? Sure have missed seeing your pretty face around here."

"Aww, you're nothing but a big old flirt, Jim Colton. How've *you* been? And how're Bessie and those two beautiful girls of yours?"

He'd always called me "little girl". I'm not sure why, although I am kind of on the small side at slightly under five-one on a tall day, and I am a girl. I smiled back. Something about Big Jim always made people smile.

His wife Bessie had suffered a pretty significant stroke a few years ago, and though she could walk a little with assistance, she spent most of her time confined to a wheelchair. Her cognition remained intact, but her speech had been severely affected, and she waged a constant struggle to communicate. But, she and Jim had some secret language of their own, because he always knew exactly what she tried to say, and he was the one who could always make her laugh no matter how frustrated she became. Between his salary, his extra shifts, and Bessie's disability check, they struggled every month to make ends meet and keep their two daughters in the community college. But, you would never know Big Jim had a care in the world. No matter how tough things got, he always had a smile and a kind word, and he never, ever complained.

"Well, Bessie is Bessie, you know," he said fondly. "Our Tanya graduated last month and is working as a paralegal downtown for that law office you see on the TV all the time, and Tammy's still working on her graphic design degree. Should be done next summer. I sure am proud of those baby girls."

"And you hide it so well," I teased. If he puffed up

any bigger, he might burst.

"So you all dolled up for that doctor of yours?" he teased right back.

"I'm not dolled up, and he's not my doctor anymore, Jim."

"Pffft...some men don't have a brain in their head no matter how many letters they got after their name," he observed astutely.

True story. Told you Jim could always make me smile. After eliciting his promise to give Bessie my regards, I waved goodbye and made my way through the lobby and down the industrially carpeted hallway to the elevator.

Roger's office was on the third floor, and I could have gotten there blindfolded. The waiting room was empty, but the rhythmic tapping I heard over the softly piped in muzak told me someone was in the office. I rapped on the glass partition, and the pointed, pixyish face of Debbie Sims, the office transcriptionist, peeked around the doorway of the inner office.

"Hey, Max," she grinned. "C'mon back." She buzzed me in and tore off her headphones to wrap me in a big, welcoming hug.

Again I say, it's good to be missed.

Debbie wasn't much taller than me, but her loud voice and ebullient personality always made her seem much bigger. No one ever called *her* little girl. She'd always been a real hoot to work with.

"So where is everyone?" I looked around nonchalantly.

"Everyone?"

"Okay," I lowered my voice to a whisper. "Specifically, Barb. I heard she was running the office after I left."

"Oh my God, Max, you really need to get out more. She hasn't been here in over a year. It was only a stop gap until the temp agency could find someone for the long term. She went back to Florida months ago, as soon as Doc finalized his plans for Somalia."

By the tone of Debbie's voice, I got the distinct impression the temp agency couldn't come up with someone fast enough to suit her and get Barbie out of the picture. And what was this months ago thing? Roger had said she was in South Beach on vacation, right? Or did he? It was all mixed up in my head. Maybe something to do with the huge stapled gash I was nursing the night we'd had the conversation.

"I still can't believe you thought she and Doc...you know what? Never mind, it is so none of my business."

"No, it's okay Debbie," I replied a little stiffly, my smile frozen in place. "You obviously have an opinion, so go ahead, and let me have it."

"Fine, but remember you asked for it," she warned. "When I found out you were leaving Roger, I was stunned. I never saw it coming. But later, when I found out the reason was you saw him at that restaurant and actually believed...well, let me just say, I struggled for a long time trying to decide whether you are that stupid or that insecure. I finally decided you've always appeared to be reasonably intelligent. Well, at least I thought you were reasonably intelligent until I realized you had apparently divorced me right along with Roger."

The hurt in her voice came through loud and clear. And I guess she had every right to feel that way. Debbie and I had worked together for a long time. We were good friends. We'd laughed together, lunched together, and confided in one another for years. When I left Roger, I left the office, I left it all. For one thing, I hadn't wanted to put her in the middle, and for another it had simply hurt too much.

"Debbie, I..." I began.

"It is *so* good to see you," she interrupted enthusiastically, punctuating the pronouncement with another tight squeeze that left me gasping for air and unable to finish what I had been about to say. "You look fantastic! Doesn't she look great, Doc?"

I hadn't heard the door open behind me, but when I turned, Roger stood there with an odd expression on his face. I wondered uncomfortably how much he'd overheard.

"Max always looks good," he agreed pleasantly.

Don't say it, Max, don't say, don't say it.

"So I don't look any better right now than I did the other night in a hospital gown with blood-matted hair?"

Damn, I'd said it. Remember that ninety-nine percent chance if there is a thought in my head, it will be exiting through my mouth? I told you, I'm working on it.

"Fishing, Max?" He flashed me a knowing smile. I may as well have called him ahead of time to see what he wanted me to wear.

"Biting, Rog?" I smiled as sweetly as my grinding teeth would allow.

"Sure, why not?" He laughed infuriatingly. "Okay, yes, you look much nicer today than you did in a hospital gown with blood-matted hair. Happy? Now, are you ready? I have office hours in about twenty minutes."

Roger's office hadn't changed much since the last time I'd been in it. His grandfather's dark, oak desk still hogged the spotlight. A wall of textbooks and medical reference manuals on shelves behind it provided stripes of color that contrasted nicely with the high, cushioned back of his black leather chair. The carpeting was a typical industrial looking office type in a neutral shade of dark gray. The spider plant I'd bought him when he moved in was still on the windowsill, its tentacles spilling down the wall and onto the floor. I did notice one change. The framed photo of the two of us on vacation at Niagara Falls that had always had a prominent place on his desk was absent. Well, what had I expected, a shrine?

I took a seat in one of the two wingback chairs, across the desk from Roger, and crossed my legs waiting for him to get comfortable. He pulled a folder from a stack on his right and flipped it open. He shuffled through the thick contents for a minute and pulled several sheets free and laid them on top of the rest. He turned the folder around and slid it across the desk toward me along with a pen he'd taken from the breast pocket of his white lab coat. It was a slim gold design engraved with his initials that I'd given him for our fifth anniversary.

"I won't waste your time having you read through all of this, unless, of course you don't trust me to summarize?"

"I have no problem with your veracity when it comes to business matters, Roger. Summarize away."

"Okay, essentially, in the event something should happen to me, this gives you full legal access to all of my business accounts and records, and full authorization to make whatever decisions you need to, related to the practice, up to and including its sale." He pointed to a signature line at the bottom of the first page. He had already signed.

I scribbled my signature, and he flipped to the next. "This transfers ownership of the condo, the car, and all personal property, accounts, and investments to you in the event of my death."

My gaze flew to his face. I didn't really appreciate his terminology. I did not want to sign anything that related to "in the event of his death". I was superstitious that way. Sure, I looked forward to my alimony check every month as much as the next unemployed divorcee, but I had plenty. I didn't need the rest. I didn't want to ever think of him in that dreary bus terminal with Marvin Jenks. I made a mental note to buy him a copy of Kubler-Ross for Christmas.

"Roger," I said uneasily, setting down the pen and wiping my suddenly moist palms on the sides of my slacks. "What exactly are you getting yourself into?"

"Delivering care in Somalia is challenging, Max. I'm going in with an established organization on a humanitarian aid mission, but the terrorists aren't all that discriminating. The healthcare and aid workers routinely receive threats and intimidation from insurgents in both the south and central areas of the country. It's a volatile area and anything could happen. I'm sure I'll be fine, but there are no guarantees, and I need to make sure things are in order, just in case."

"Why me? We're divorced now. I shouldn't be the one making these decisions. What about your parents?"

"You know they aren't up to any of this in the event it becomes necessary. It's just a simple matter of getting everything legally spelled out, and I've drafted a living will, as well. Don't worry, Max, much as you may want to, it won't be you pulling the plug if it comes to it."

"That's a rotten thing to say, Roger. I know we've had our differences, but that doesn't mean I wish you dead. Just because we aren't married anymore doesn't mean I don't care about you."

Take that, pal. Eat those words. Put that in your pipe and smoke it.

I couldn't even let my mind wander to a place where Roger lay in that bed instead of Gerri. Could not do it.

"Sign the papers, Max." He sighed. "I'll have my lawyer make copies and get them to you when everything is processed. In a nutshell, if anything happens to me, everything goes to you, aside from a separate provision for my parents. Gee, almost like we're still married, huh?"

"Give me the damn papers," I groused, and added my signature on every line he indicated. I pushed the pile toward him and sat back, my hands gripping the arms of the chair so he wouldn't notice how they trembled. "When do you leave?"

Roger gathered the papers together, tapped them against the top of his desk into a neat stack, and returned them to the folder. He glanced at his watch, and settled back in the chair. "Sunday."

"So soon?"

"Max, I've been planning this for almost two years. It shouldn't come as any big surprise."

"I guess not. I just thought..." I thought he would never actually go. I thought he would give up the idea of heading into a third world country in the throes of civil unrest. He'd started talking about it shortly after the heartbreaking day we were forced to accept we would never have children. We'd both grieved the loss of that dream.

When we received the final verdict, instead of letting him envelope me in his arms to share our disappointment as he did after every negative test, every failed treatment, every little pee stick that didn't turn blue, I decided I didn't need anyone, not even him. Once I knew it was hopeless, once I knew I was the defective piece of the fertility puzzle, I'd wrapped myself in my pain and my failure as a wife and retreated into a solitary shell of misery.

I knew in my heart he'd eventually grow tired of a malfunctioning wife, find someone new, and have the family he wanted so badly. Roger, on the other hand, had thrown himself into his work and started talking about humanitarian missions. So, I wallowed deeper and nursed my pain while I awaited the inevitable. For the first time, it occurred to me that maybe I actually had pushed him away. I guess sometimes you have to step back from the frame in order to see the big picture. Self-sabotage, the other white meat.

A discreet knock on the door broke into my suddenly contemplative silence. Roger's office nurse, Carol, stuck her head in.

"Doctor? Mrs. Logan, your one forty-five is here."

"I'll be out in a few minutes, Carol, thanks."

"Mrs. Logan?" I looked at him blankly. To the best of my knowledge, mine is the only Logan family in the county. Therefore, the only Mrs. Logan it could possibly be was Gail. What was Gail doing here and why hadn't she mentioned she was seeing Roger?

"Gail? What's Gail doing here?"

"This from the girl who invoked HIPAA against me in the ER? You know I can't tell you that, Max. Besides, even if I could, Gail asked me not to mention it to anyone," Roger said, watching me with quiet expectancy.

"Well, you had to know I would run into her here today," I accused, and then the light bulb came on. "You planned it!"

He shrugged, but one corner of his lips tugged upward in a half smile. "I vehemently deny it, of course, but if you should happen to run into her here in the office...oh, well! I can't take any responsibility for coincidence. I didn't tell you, right? I know she isn't your favorite person, but I didn't have any excuse to get your sister or your father here, and knowing Gail, I figured if she was worried enough to make an appointment, she might be in need of some emotional support."

He set the folder aside and pushed back from the desk. He rose to his feet, stretching his arms over his head to loosen his back. Then he rolled his shoulders and rotated his head with a groan. He was always stiff after a morning in surgery.

"And when you think of emotional support you naturally think of me?" He didn't bother to answer. Sometimes silence speaks louder than words. "Actually," I continued, "I've been thinking lately maybe I haven't given Gail enough credit over the years. She isn't so bad."

I couldn't miss the imperceptible widening of his eyes in surprise. I also couldn't miss the lines at the corners of his mouth, etched more deeply than I remembered, his movements slower and seeming forced. He looked tired, and not the kind of tired a good night's sleep or a couple of days at the beach would cure.

"Roger, are you okay?" I asked quietly.

"What? Oh, yeah... just tired. How's your head by the way?"

"Seems to be okay...staples will come out next week, I hope."

"Glad to hear it. You were lucky."

"Yep, that's my middle name."

He walked around the desk and held out a hand to pull me out of the chair. We were only inches apart and he released my hand slowly. I looked into his eyes and couldn't even comprehend there was a possibility he wouldn't come back.

Yes, I'd left him, and yes we went months without seeing one another. But, even if I'd left him, even if he found someone else, even if he didn't love me anymore, at least I always knew he existed somewhere in the world and as long as he did, there was always the possibility...

"Roger, be careful over there, okay? Be really, really, careful."

He smiled briefly, and I thought he would say something more, but then he seemed to think better of it and turned me toward the door.

"C'mon, Lucky, let's go find your stepmother."

****

Carol was just bringing Gail back to an exam room as Roger and I stepped out of his office and into the hallway. Dressed in crisp, beige, linen Capri pants and a short sleeved, white, silk blouse, she looked tailored, cool, and fresh. But, what worried me was the fact that her pronounced palor made it difficult to tell where the blouse ended and Gail began. I knew by the way Roger started that he'd noticed it too.

"Gail! What are you doing here?" I adopted my best I-didn't-know-a-thing-about-this-party voice.

Yeah, that one.

And no, she wasn't fooled for a second. Her brows came together in a scowl reminiscent of Unibrow the Boy Wonder. At least it was aimed at Roger and not at me.

"Roger, you promised!"

"Hi Gail. Max just stopped by to sign some papers. I've been hounding her to do it for weeks. Actually, I forgot you even had an appointment today. Some coincidence, huh?" Roger opened his brown eyes wide and spread his hands in front of him palm up, the universal sign language gesture for "who me". Her look said she wasn't buying that, either.

"Yeah, I've been so busy, it was the first chance I had to stop by. So, what are you doing here? Dad didn't mention you were coming to see Roger."

"He doesn't know and neither does your sister, and I'd like to keep it that way. Busy, my ass, Maxine," she snapped in a very uncharacteristic Stepmother Gail manner. "You hole up in that apartment and do nothing but feel sorry for yourself and bite everyone's head off with your scintillating sarcasm. You don't work, you don't socialize, and if you didn't need to go to the SuperSave for food every now and then, I'm afraid we'd find your mummified corpse in a pink mouse night shirt curled up on your couch one of these days."

Well, sure it sounded bad when she said it like that!
I thought she was being kind of harsh considering just this week alone I'd died, discovered a body, bequeathed a million dollars to a woman in a coma, helped a man come to terms with losing the love of his life, given a wayward granddaughter a twelfth second chance at a decent life, and acknowledged maybe I'd been partially responsible for the break-up of my marriage. Now, here I was trying to be the Rock of Gibraltar for Stepmother Gail who I'd also recently decided might not be the root of all evil. And it was only Monday. Who says I'm not busy?

Gail's acrimonious attitude worried me even more. It was so completely out of character for her that I knew she was either deeply worried or incredibly afraid. Roger was a big help. It seemed he had trouble picking his jaw up from the floor following her tirade. I nudged him with my elbow. Jump in anytime here, cowboy! Nope, he wasn't doing it. No comment was forthcoming from the peanut gallery.

"Gail, I truly did come in to sign some papers. Roger didn't tell me anything, he only mentioned I might run into you right as I was leaving. Now, why don't you tell me what's going on? If you don't want me to say anything to Dad and Denise, my lips are sealed, but it's obvious you aren't feeling well, and I'd like to help if I can, even if all I can offer is moral support." I swallowed hard. "You've always been there for me."

Gail heroically managed to keep her own jaw from hitting the floor when I added the last, even as her face crumpled. It occurred to me I had never actually seen Gail cry, at least not in public.

Hmm, maybe I took after her? Nature versus nurture?

I put an arm around her shoulders, and she leaned into me as her breath came in muffled sobs and the tears trickled down her pale cheeks. Roger nodded toward the exam room, and I guided her in the right direction. I pried her handbag from her stiff fingers, and claimed the chair in the corner as Roger helped her onto the exam table and pulled up a stool. He scribbled on a prescription pad, tore off the top sheet, and handed it to Carol. Then he glanced at the results when the nurse finished checking Gail's pulse and blood pressure.

"Why don't you start at the beginning, Gail," he encouraged kindly, placing a hand on her knee. I was relieved to see Gail had regained some of her normal composure by this time, and she launched into her account of rectal bleeding that had apparently been going on for weeks. Lately, she'd begun to feel weak and tired all the time. She thought it would stop, but it was getting worse instead of better. She was afraid she had cancer. My stomach felt queasy. I was afraid she might be right. She had been carrying this around alone for weeks, and for most of that time I'd been my usual charming self. Wow, can't imagine why she didn't feel like she could confide in me.

Roger asked her a multitude of questions, and then handed Gail a stylish paper gown and asked me to step outside while Carol drew blood, and Roger conducted his exam. When he finished, he opened the door and motioned me back in.

"What do you think?" I asked as Gail clutched my hand like a lifeline. Roger looked over the lab results, scribbled a little more, and then closed the file.

"Well, I know you didn't want Dan and Denise to know anything, Gail, but I don't think you have a choice. Normal hemoglobin for a woman is twelve to sixteen. Yours is six point five and your blood pressure is also running low. It's no wonder you've been feeling tired and weak. You are definitely losing blood and we need to find out why. I'd like to admit you today, transfuse you with a couple of units of packed cells to get your counts up, and start a bowel prep in anticipation of a colonoscopy and some other tests tomorrow. Once I can get in there and have a look, I'll have a much better idea of what we're dealing with and what we're going to do about it. How does that sound?" He said all this with a smile as calm and genuine as if he'd just offered Gail an appetizer with her martini.

"Well," she looked from me, to Roger, to me again. "What do you think I should do, Max?"

"I think you should do whatever Roger tells you to do. He's the best."

"Roger," she began in a trembling voice. "Do you think it's something serious?"

"I think it can be any number of things, Gail. Some of them serious, yes, but many more of them not such a big deal, and easily treated. I know it's difficult, but try not to worry too much until we find out if there is anything to worry about."

I searched his face, looking for some hint of what he was thinking, and he simply winked. I thought his confidence alone could make a person believe in miracles. No wonder his patients loved him.

"I'm going to call the hospital transport service to pick you up here and take you over to be admitted so you don't have to walk. They can take you right from the medical arts building, through the tunnel, and into admissions in a wheelchair. Max can go over with you and call Denise to pick up some things for you at home, if you'd like. Maybe Denise can even pick Dan up on her way over, and then he can drive your car home. If not, it should be fine in the lot overnight. I still have a few patients to see this afternoon but I'll stop in to see you before I leave for the day and see how you're doing, okay?"

"Okay," she agreed with a shaky smile. Roger and I stepped out to allow Gail some privacy while she got dressed. As soon as the door closed behind me, I began to shake like a dog in the rain. I clutched at the back of Roger's lab coat as I felt my knees buckle. He turned in time to catch me and hold me steady.

"Hey," he said softly. "What's this?"

"Sorry." I laughed in a shaky voice. I stepped back and he seemed almost reluctant to let me go. Of course, that had to be my imagination, or maybe wishful thinking, since I knew I'd been nothing but a bitch on wheels for months on end. It must have been his Hippocratic Oath kicking in. First, do no harm, second, keep ex-wives from making a splat on your office floor.

"I guess this upset me a little more than I thought. I looked at her while we were sitting in there. I mean actually looked at her. God, Roger, when did she get old? She looks so pale and feeble. Level with me, do you think it could be cancer?" I'd already lost my mother to cancer. I couldn't lose Gail, too.

"I told you what I think. I can't rule anything out completely until I get in there, but she hasn't been losing weight, and she hasn't had any noticeable changes in her bowel movements, so I'm cautiously optimistic. Don't get yourself all worked up until we know if there's anything to get all worked up about, okay? Actually, I have to say I'm a little surprised you're so upset."

"Yeah, me, too. Things change, I guess. People change."

"You don't do change, remember?" Roger laughed. "I think I saw it carved in stone somewhere."

"Well, sometimes you don't have much of a choice." I sighed. "Sometimes karma just sneaks up and kicks you in the butt."

Or smacks your head off of the floor of an Italian marble shower stall complete with a Chastings Corque Corian Square Ceiling Mount Showerhead.

****

I had a new appreciation for Roger as a doctor. He took care of everything. He even had Gail laughing and joking by the time hospital transport arrived. Within forty minutes, Gail was assessed, admitted, gowned, and sitting up in bed watching the tail end of her favorite soap opera on the tiny, little TV screen that swung out from the wall on a folding metal bracket.

Roger had not so accidentally let slip that Gail was his mother-in-law, not bothering to precede it with the ex, and so we were in a spacious private room with bright, sunny windows, and furnished with two vinyl reclining chairs in addition to the standard hospital bed.

A pleasant, young nurse had come in as soon as Gail got settled and took yet more blood. We were currently waiting for the type and cross-match to be completed so they could start the blood transfusion. In the meantime, a plastic bag of five percent dextrose dripped through the tubing into Gail's left hand, while she poked unhappily at a delicious looking bowl of yellow gelatin, since they had immediately placed her on a liquid diet.

I'd called both Dad and Denise from Roger's office earlier. Dad planned to come over later tonight after he closed the store. He wanted to come right away, but once I put Roger on the phone and he assured Dad there was no imminent danger, he allowed himself to be convinced to wait, especially after I promised to stay until either he or Denise arrived. Denise, on the other hand, reacted with borderline hysteria, which went a long way toward putting me back in my Rock of Gibraltar mode.

I was just contrary like that. No one needed to know I suffered a little emotional blip earlier. Of course, Roger knew, but if he felt any compulsion to mention it to anyone, I planned to invoke my right to doctor-patient confidentiality. Okay, maybe he wasn't exactly *my* doctor, but he was a smart guy. He had enough self-preservation instincts to recognize a veiled threat when he heard one.

My good friend, caffeine, was calling my name. I ignored him as long as I could, but finally, after making sure Gail was comfortable and could easily reach the little red nurse call button, I left her engrossed in an afternoon talk show and set off in search of a vending machine. One awaited my attention in the visitors' lounge at the end of the hall, and I dropped my coins in and waited for the cup to fill. It looked like coffee, it smelled like coffee, but I knew from past experience that unless I cultivated an active fantasy of Juan Valdez riding in on a burro with every sip, it tasted like something closer to dishwater latte. But, it was better than nothing, barely. I dropped another buck and a quarter into the beverage machine and got Gail a bottle of apple juice. I didn't know if she actually liked apple juice, but I figured at this point, most any liquid on the planet had to trump yellow hospital gelatin.

I'd just passed the nurses' station when I heard someone call my name. I groaned internally as I recognized the distinctive aroma of Dirk Kramer. The man wore enough cologne to induce an asthma attack. Dirk is one of those more is better kind of guys, and eschewed the notion of discreetly applying cologne in favor of marinating in it. In his seven-hundred dollar Italian cut suits, gold watch, and gleaming Italian loafers, Dirk fancies himself a ladies' man. And maybe he is, but I think it's highly dependent on your definition of a lady.

The nurses avoided him like the plague. He'd been hitting on me, and anything else with breasts, for the better part of ten years. It hadn't mattered that I had a husband. Of course, why should it? He has a wife. He is, in a word, scum. I'd always struggled to be polite in the face of his overtly inappropriate behavior while I was married, since he was a colleague of Roger's and I didn't want to put him in an awkward position. Poor Dirk, he thought it was to his advantage that I wasn't married anymore.

"Max," he called cheerfully. "How've you been? I've just come from seeing your stepmother. Lovely woman."

I squared my shoulders and turned slowly back to where he emerged from the dictation area behind the desk. "Why?" I responded as politely as possible.

"Why, what?

"Why did you see Gail?" I bit out each word slowly and carefully.

When dealing with children, use small words and enunciate carefully.

"Oh." He tossed a chart on the desk and came out into the hallway where I clutched Gail's apple juice. "Well, I guess you didn't know I'll be covering Roger's caseload while he's out of the country. You do know he's going to Somalia?"

"I do actually, Dirk. But I also know he isn't leaving until Sunday, so I don't see any reason for you to be involved in the case at this point."

"You know me, Max." He winked, I shuddered. "I like to stay on top of things."

His gaze strayed to a few of the things he liked to stay on top of, and I forked two fingers in the direction of my eyes. "Hey, Dirk, I'm up here."

The nurses were glued to our exchange, though they managed to look busy and pretend otherwise. That remark earned me an enthusiastic thumbs up.

"Aw c'mon, Max," he wheedled, stepping closer.

I just as quickly took a step back. "Back off, Dirk," I demanded. "This is my dance space." I held my arms out in a semicircle, then gestured in his general direction. "That is your dance space."

He had the audacity, or maybe it was the stupidity, to laugh. "Oh, Max, I do love a woman with sass. Roger is a great guy, but we both know he was never man enough for a woman like you. And now that you finally realized it, too…" he waggled his brows and left the sentence dangling.

His meaning was clear. Subtlety was never one of Dirk's strong points. Frankly, I couldn't believe he'd never been hit with a sexual harassment suit.

I will not be sarcastic, I will not be sarcastic, I will not be sarcastic. Oh, who am I kidding?

"You are absolutely right, Dirk," I cooed suggestively, and his eyes widened in disbelieving anticipation as I stepped closer. His lips parted in an oily grin. I let him enjoy his expected score for about ten seconds, and then my voice hardened and the gloves came off. "Roger *is* a great guy, and he's also twice the man you could ever hope to be. Now, only because I've always been a strong proponent of helping the less fortunate, let me give you a complimentary lesson in how *not* to pick me up. First, don't assume I'm flattered. I'm not. Second, don't be a rude, crude, sexually desperate ass-hat. I realize that will take a great deal of practice on your part. You may be cute, but underneath that pretty exterior you are nothing but slime, and there isn't a popsicle's chance in hell I will ever sleep with you. I hope you appreciate that in the interest of our long and professional relationship, I have attempted to spare your ego with my kind and understated refusal, even though you are a complete toad. No need to thank me. You're welcome. Any questions?"

I batted my big blues flirtatiously, a gesture he couldn't possibly miss as his eyes were now definitely locked on my face, instead of my water bra-assisted cleavage, with a look of horror and confounded humiliation. All sounds of activity behind him had ceased, and we had the undivided attention of every nurse at the desk. Phones rang, lights buzzed, faxes rolled, but every woman there had paused in pregnant anticipation of his response.

I watched with a sense of complete satisfaction as his mouth dropped open and his eyes bulged comically.

Hey, my toad analogy was spot on. Who knew?

Dirk Kramer had finally run out of witty come-ons. He didn't even seem able to muster a pathetic comeback. I guess my gracious declination had left him speechless. He spun on the heel of his designer shoes and stalked off down the hallway and around the corner without a single backward glance.

I turned in the direction of Gail's room with a triumphant smile, and swore I caught two nurses engaging in a high five out of the corner of my eye. I could have been mistaken. But, there was no mistaking the smattering of applause that followed my swaggering retreat.

Gail was pitifully grateful for the apple juice. It turns out most any liquid on the planet really does trump yellow gelatin.

Chapter Ten

While Gail morosely drank her dinner, I decided to risk another hike to the vending machines to see what I could rustle up in the way of a nutritious meal. I figured it would be a toss-up between potato chips and chocolate. As luck would have it, Denise chose that propitious moment to appear in the doorway with enough baggage for a European World Tour, juggling it madly, like a bell boy on crack.

"Denise." I couldn't help laughing. "This is a hospital not a hotel. Your mom is having tests, not moving in."

"You never know what you might need," she returned, crossing the room to dump everything in the vinyl recliner I had recently vacated. She hurried to the bedside and immediately burst into tears.

"For heaven's sake, Denise, don't overreact," Gail admonished testily. "Roger isn't worried, and so neither am I. It's only a few tests and then he'll take care of whatever it is."

"Is that what he said?" Denise's watery gaze swiveled to me.

"More or less," I confirmed. "He said we shouldn't worry until we find out if there's a reason to, and he's cautiously optimistic it isn't anything serious."

Her eyes narrowed. "And you believe him?"

"Of course I do, why wouldn't I?"

She quirked a brow meaningfully.

"For heaven's sake, Denise, that's an entirely different thing. Roger is an excellent doctor and a fundamentally honest man."

"*I* know that," Denise replied, rising to unpack. "I'm just surprised to hear *you* say it. Of course, you weren't exactly in your right mind at the time."

"And what's that supposed to mean," I demanded, snagging a bag out of her hand and turning to fold the five pairs of pajamas in five different fabrics and colors into the built in chest of drawers. I thought *they* were a bit much until I located the five pairs of bedroom slippers and three robes underneath. Talk about people not in their right minds. When it came to packing, Denise had gone over the edge.

"Hey, you were going through a lot back then and, let's face it, you aren't always the easiest person in the world." Denise started on a second bag.

I didn't even own as many bath products as Denise apparently felt were essential for a hospital stay. Gail didn't either. When Denise is upset, Denise goes shopping.

"Are you referring back to your comment the other day about me pushing people away? Are you implying I pushed Roger into cheating? That it's *my* fault?" Just because the same thought had briefly occurred to me once or twice lately did not mean I wanted to hear anyone, least of all my own sister, agreed with it. From her vantage point in the bed, Gail avidly sucked on her straw, apparently having forgotten she hates grapefruit juice, her head swiveling back and forth between us like a spectator at a tennis match.

Denise emptied the last bag and closed the drawer.

Then she turned and leaned back against the counter and sighed. "No, of course not, Max. I don't think there's ever an excuse for infidelity. But, *I* know Roger to be an honest guy. You've said *you* know Roger to be an honest guy. What I'm saying is you weren't yourself, then. Maybe you did push him away, but, maybe the way you were feeling about your loss and your marriage and yourself in general had you feeling…well, I don't know…but, maybe those feelings colored your perception of what really happened that night."

"Maybe." Or maybe I knew he was too honorable to leave a barren wife. Maybe I feared his love would someday turn to resentment and a feeling of having been cheated, and I didn't think I could bear watching that happen. Maybe I thought he deserved the chance to have a child of his own with someone who could give it to him. There were a lot of maybes. I wasn't sure even I knew the truth anymore. About a lot of things. If a grudge exists only in my own mind, is it still a grudge? I wondered if one of my heretofore untapped SSI superpowers was the ability to elicit unsolicited and insightful observations from my sister. Frankly, it was starting to make me uncomfortable.

"No more psych classes for you," I warned Denise in my best Soup Nazi voice.

Before she could respond, there were footsteps outside and in walked Roger. He nodded to Denise and me, but went right to the bedside.

"How're you feeling?" he asked Gail.

"Not too bad…though the meals leave a lot to be desired," she replied with a disgusted look at the half finished broth and yet another hefty serving of jiggling yellow cubes.

"I can see that," he laughed. "I just checked your chart and the type and cross is back so they should be getting the packed cells up from the blood bank shortly. You'll be amazed at how much better you'll feel once you get some blood in you. They'll start the bowel prep after dinner. It's not painful, but it's not fun. Unfortunately, it's a necessary evil. We'll do the colonoscopy first thing in the morning and with any luck, you'll have a much more appetizing lunch tomorrow."

"Well, tonight doesn't sound like much fun, but I'll try to stay focused on the prospect of a solid lunch." Gail tried to smile.

"You do that," Roger replied, patting her hand. "I'll see you first thing in the morning."

My stomach growled loudly to remind me I'd never made it back to the vending machine.

"Denise, are you staying a while? Dad should be here soon. I thought maybe I'd head out."

"Yeah, I'll be here. The girls are at a friend's house and Brad will pick them up on his way home. You go on. I still can't believe Mom told you about this and not me," she gave Gail a reproachful look. "I bet Dad knew, too."

"Stop pouting, Denise. She didn't tell anyone," I snapped, returning the look. "I just happened to run into her at Roger's office and the jig was up."

"Well, as Roger says, there isn't any point in worrying about something until you know if you have something to worry about," Gail countered. "So there wasn't any reason to tell anyone anything. And now you know, so stop harassing the patient."

She might say that now, but I'd seen her earlier and she hadn't only been worried, she'd been terrified, and still she'd kept it to herself, probably building it up into a death sentence in her head, rather than upset the people she cared about.

"Are you leaving now, Max?" Roger asked then said before I could answer, "I'll walk you out. Your car is next door, right? I have to stop at the office for a minute anyway, so I'm headed that way."

"Oh, uh, yeah, sure," I stammered. Denise started humming Abba's *Mama Mia,* and I was hard pressed to refrain from smacking her in the head. I settled for pressing a kiss to Gail's papery cheek, which seemed to surprise everyone including me, and telling her I would see her in the morning. I hugged my sister and told her to call me if there was any change and then turned toward Roger who was waiting inside the door. He'd just stepped back to let me pass when Gail called my name.

"Maxine?"

"Yeah?" I turned back.

"I'm glad you were here," she said quietly. "Thank you."

"You're welcome," I smiled back. "I am, too." And, surprisingly, I realized I meant it.

****

We had to pass the nurses' station on our way to the elevators. All of the nurses still at the desk looked up and gave me conspiratorial smiles as we approached. One gave me a thumbs up.

"Epic, Mrs. McCoy, simply epic!" a petite blonde in pink scrubs and a perky ponytail called out as we passed.

"Mrs. McCoy?" Roger raised a brow.

I flushed. Not everyone knew I'd reverted to my maiden name. I mean, it wasn't like I'd taken out a full page newspaper ad or anything. "Happy to provide an entertaining respite, ladies." I laughed and gave a mock bow.

"Am I missing something here, Paula?" Roger addressed the ponytail, leaning an elbow on the desk and crossing his ankles casually. Behind him, I shook my head frantically at bubbly, blonde Paula. She either didn't notice or didn't understand. Maybe it was a blonde thing.

"Well, let's just say Dr. Kramer will think twice before he hits on your wife...er, ex-wife again!" Paula laughed and the others joined in appreciatively.

"Really..." Roger drawled, looking around at me with my head in mid shake. "Do tell." He looked back at Paula who'd finally interpreted my sign language.

"Uh, well there was something about a sexually desperate ass-hat, a popsicle's chance in hell, oh, and an unflattering comparison to a toad, I think. I don't remember, exactly. But he definitely had it coming," she finished with an emphatic bob of her ponytail.

"A sexually desperate ass-hat, Max?" he choked out, trying to maintain a serious expression and failing miserably.

"You know me, Roger. Call 'em like I see 'em." I smiled cheekily. "That's how I roll."

"And the popsicle's chance in hell?"

"Um, that would be the likelihood of his getting me into bed." He did laugh then, a deep, hearty laugh of pure enjoyment I hadn't heard in ages. I couldn't suppress the grin that split my face in return. He shook his head, coughing.

"Maxine Esmeralda Logan McCoy, sometimes you are positively priceless."

"Esmeralda?" I heard a giggle from somewhere behind the desk.

"Family name," I muttered, rolling my eyes at Roger and stomping off in the direction of the elevators.

Isn't Esme the name of one of those sparkly vampires everyone is so obsessed with these days? What do you think that's short for? Harvey? You don't hear anyone laughing at her do you?

Roger was still shaking his head and chuckling when he joined me in the elevator. He waited until the others on the elevator got off on the second floor before commenting. "I've heard rumors Kramer can be...er, inappropriate. Guess he figured you're fair game now that we're divorced," he observed. "He apparently didn't know who he was dealing with. *Sexually desperate ass-hat*...good one, Max." And he began chuckling again.

"He's a pig, Roger. And my being available had nothing to do with it. First of all, even if I am, he's not. Secondly he's been hitting on me, and anything that's breathing, for years. I felt like I had to be semi-polite when we were married because he was a colleague of yours. Dirk made the mistake of thinking I would continue to afford him that courtesy, I guess."

"He hit on you when we were married? Why didn't you ever say anything?" he asked tightly.

"Sure, he did. I didn't feel special, he hits on everyone. I guess maybe he figures the law of averages is in his favor and someone will eventually take him up on it, though frankly I'm not sure the dipwad would know what to do about it if anyone ever did. I never said anything because it didn't seem necessary to say anything. I could handle him, and I didn't want to put you in a difficult situation. Don't worry about it, Roger, I doubt he'll be approaching me again anytime soon."

I pictured the look on Dirk Kramer's face after my little speech and couldn't help smiling again. The hospital grapevine was notorious. I had no doubt that by tomorrow at the latest, everyone would have heard about my run in with Dirk Kramer, word for word, and he knew it. Maybe it would make him think twice before inflicting his unwanted attentions on anyone else, at least for a while. Maybe.

Most of the offices in the medical arts building were closed and the connecting tunnel was nearly deserted at this time of day. The sharp click of my heels on the tile was the only sound as we walked side by side in companionable silence. I didn't wear heels much anymore and I certainly hadn't left the house today with the intention of spending all day in them. My feet were killing me. Leather straps and stilettos are not my friends. I concentrated on camouflaging my limp until we reached the lobby where Big Jim remained at his station, still glued to the monitors. He must be working a double again.

"Well," I began as Roger hesitated near the hallway to the elevator. "I, uh, guess I'll see you in the morning? What time did you schedule Gail's test for?"

"Seven-thirty. I'll see what we've got and take it from there. If possible, I'd like to have her squared away before I leave on Sunday. I'd rather not hand her case over to anyone, especially now." He frowned darkly.

"I appreciate that, Roger. And, um, thanks for everything today. So, I guess I'll see you in the morning, then." I began to turn away toward the door to the parking lot where I'd left my car. Surprising me, Roger began to walk along with me. I looked through the glass and noticed an attractive, well-dressed woman standing outside the door. Her eyes were fixed on me as I approached. A vague and fuzzy golden nimbus surrounded her like faint, flickering flames, and when I looked over Big Jim's shoulder, it said something about what my life had become since my death when I wasn't the least bit surprised she didn't show up on his monitor. I turned to Roger to say good-bye and surprised a wistful look on his face.

"Max, um, I have a history and physical to dictate on a patient I admitted this afternoon, but it should only take a couple of minutes. Neither of us has eaten yet…do you, uh…want to grab a burger or something?" he offered hesitantly.

I realized I would actually love to grab a burger, or something, with Roger, but there was a tiki torch on the other side of the door and I had no doubt she was waiting for me. I felt a little niggle of unease. She was definitely not a ghost, and I wondered if maybe I should have been a little less insistent in regards to sticking my nose into Ernie's unfinished business. Maybe my part of the bargain didn't include inflicting my opinions on the corporeally challenged?

"I, uh…I can't, Roger," I began regretfully and a shutter slid into place over his expression. He nodded shortly and began to turn away. "I'm, uh, sorry…I can't tonight, but I'll take a rain check if you're offering?"

"Sure." He smiled slowly. "I'll see you in the

morning, then. Be careful driving home."

"Always am." I smiled back nervously. "G'night."

I watched Roger as he strode back toward the elevator and his office. I hoped he was right and I would see him in the morning. I hoped I wasn't about to find out I'd screwed up and Marvin had sent someone to tell me our bargain was null and void. I hoped tomorrow morning I would be sitting in the surgical waiting room with the people I loved, and not in an unsanitary bus terminal with Marvin Jenks. I hoped this wasn't goodbye. Only one way to find out. I took a deep, steadying breath, and after wishing Big Jim a good evening and reminding him to give my best to Bessie, I pushed through the heavy glass to greet the neon woman waiting for me on the other side. With a surreptitious jerk of my head, I indicated she should follow me to my car. Even though Big Jim couldn't see her on the monitor, he could sure as heck see me, and it wouldn't do anything to enhance my already questionable reputation to be observed carrying on an animated conversation with myself in front of the medical arts building.

I unlocked the doors and tossed my wrinkled eco-tote, two empty water bottles, and the four pack of toilet paper I'd never bothered to take in the house into the back seat to make room. Once we were both settled with the doors closed against prying eyes and ears, I turned to her in inquiry.

"Hi, I'm Max. What can I do for you?" I stuck out a trembling hand, only slightly concerned I might get burnt. She took it and the only warmth I felt was the normal body heat of someone who had been standing out in the late day sun.

"Hi, Max, I'm Alicia Gates, the Superintendent of Spiritual Intervention. I understand you've been filling in for me the last few days." She smiled. "I'm here to tell you that effective immediately, your services will no longer be required. Thanks for your help."

"Oh, uh…sure," I stammered. "I mean, I hope I did okay. I did the best I could."

"You did fine."

"That's uh, that's great news. How's the baby?"

I mean, what else does one say to a new mother? Even if said new mother is sitting in the passenger seat of one's car glowing like a sparkler on the Fourth of July.

"She's great, thanks," Alicia the Radiant answered with a smile. "Already glimmering like a little firefly."

"Excuse me?"

"Oh, didn't Marvin explain?" Her eyes widened in surprise. "Oh well, knowing Marvin, probably not. The SSI is generally a hereditary position, runs in families as a rule. That's why your glow is more subdued than mine. Yours was manually applied for the duration of your task."

I had a glow? Huh. I looked at my arms and studied my face in the rearview mirror. Alicia laughed and it was musical.

"Oh, you can't see it, Max, any more than I can see mine. But it's there. It's how they find us."

"They?"

"Our clients, the lost, the confused, and the generally reluctant to be deceased?"

"Oh, them. Yeah, I wondered how it worked."

"Anyway, I wanted to stop by and let you know you're off the hook and to thank you for your help."

"I'm off the hook? So, I didn't mess up?" I didn't have to go back to the bus terminal? I would see Roger and my family tomorrow? I felt like Ebenezer Scrooge on Christmas morning! I felt light as a feather, happy as an angel, merry as a schoolboy! Okay, it was summer and the methodology was entirely different, but the end result was the same. I had time, I had clarity, I had my life back!

"Actually, all things considered, Max, you did pretty well." She smiled again. "It's kind of unorthodox, a non-genetic SSI, but you managed to make it work."

"Would have been nice to have a little orientation though," I groused irritably.

"Didn't you read the book?" Alicia inquired. *Life and Death are much the same. Neither comes with an instruction manual.*"

"Oh, that! Yes, that was a *huge* help...NOT!"

"Oh, Max," Alicia laughed. "Don't you see? It's really all you ever need to know. It's all about doing the best you can with what you're given. Life happens...it's your reaction that determines the outcome. Well, I'd better get going. Esmeralda will be up from her nap soon and hungry as a bear."

"Esmeralda?" I choked.

"Family name." She winked. "We call her Esme for short." Then she opened the door and climbed out and my tenure as SSI was over just as suddenly and unexpectedly as it began. I thought I'd be relieved, and I was, but there was a small part of me that was almost sad. It wasn't about losing the superpowers or anything, it was the feeling I'd had the ability to make a difference and now it was gone. But then, maybe that wasn't strictly true. Maybe I simply had to change my methods.

****

Dad, Denise, and I took turns pacing the stark confines of the endoscopy waiting area for the better part of two hours. Brad-The-Famous-Vascular-Surgeon had poked his head in between surgeries to see if we'd had any news, and my sister clung to him anxiously until he pried her away to return to the OR with a promise he would be back as soon as he could get away. I'd found a thermos under the sink at Dad's this morning, and took the time to fill it with the good stuff before we drove to the hospital. Frankly, my mind felt so scattered with anxiety I wasn't sure I could maintain the Juan Valdez fantasy long enough to get the vending machine imitation of coffee down my tight throat.

Finally, I heard voices outside at the desk and Roger strode in the door looking happy and confident in green hospital scrubs. We all jumped to our feet and surrounded him like Broadway groupies at a stage door.

"Well," he said with a happy grin. "It isn't cancer."

The room filled with the sound of three sets of lungs simultaneously releasing nervously held breaths. Dad had appeared to be the calmest of the three of us all morning, but I realized just how fragile his control, what a tight rein he'd been holding on his fear, when he sat down heavily following Roger's announcement, dropped his head into his hands, and burst into tears.

"Thank, God."

A painful spasm gripped my throat. I'd never seen Dad even close to tears before. That Rock of Gibraltar thing ran in the family. Well, except for Denise. We've already established she can whip up a deluge at the drop of a hat. But now, she swallowed hard and went to his side to put an arm around his shoulders.

"What is it?" I asked. Okay, he'd said it wasn't cancer, and that was an incredible relief, but I had to be sure we were out of the woods.

"Angiodysplasia."

"English, Roger," I demanded, and he laughed

"Sorry. Basically what we found was a collection of swollen, fragile blood vessels on the right side of Gail's colon. There are several theories about what causes this to occur, but the most likely cause is that as we age, normal spasms of the colon lead to enlargement of blood vessels in that area in some people. Sometimes the swelling becomes severe enough to cause a small direct passageway between a very small artery and vein resulting in a fistula, and that puts the patient at risk for bleeding. We found it, I cauterized it, and there doesn't appear to be any further bleeding," he concluded with a smile.

"So she's fine? It's all over?" I sighed in relief putting a hand on his arm.

"Well, I'll want to keep her overnight and recheck her blood counts in the morning. I'll also write orders at discharge for follow up blood work for the next few weeks to keep an eye on things. It's important she keep those appointments. If her blood counts hold steady, I'll want to see her in a month or so, when I get back. Angiodysplasias have been known to recur, but we know what we're dealing with and that's half the battle. We'll keep an eye on it, and she should be fine."

Dad had regained his composure and stood, offering Roger his hand. "Thank you, Roger."

"You're welcome, Dan. Glad I was able to give

you good news."

"Me, too." Dad smiled at all of us. "Can we see her now?"

"Well, she's still in recovery, but you can wait in her room if you'd like. They'll be bringing her back there, probably within the next half hour or so," Roger offered. Dad nodded and moved toward the door. Denise stopped to give Roger a heartfelt hug and followed Dad out.

"Well, this has been fun, huh?" I said with a crooked smile. "I, uh, want to thank you, too, Roger. Not only for the good news, but for, well, everything. You know, the near HIPAA violation, how great you were with Gail…everything."

"That's what families do, Max," he said quietly and my gaze flew to his face. Again. "People don't have to share DNA to be a family."

He was right. And he'd said it to me before, more than once, and under other circumstances, so I wasn't sure exactly how he meant it this time. In true Scarlett O'Hara fashion, I decided I'd worry about the ramifications of that remark tomorrow, or maybe the next day. "Hey, about that rain check," he continued in a lighter tone. "I'm going to be swamped all week, so it may have to wait until I get back from Somalia."

"Sure," I replied. "Just make sure you come back in one piece. I have no desire to negotiate with Dirk Kramer for the acquisition of your practice."

Yeah, that was my romantic way of telling him to be careful. I'm secretly an old softie like that.

I still wasn't sure if Roger had been unfaithful, but I was willing to concede I might have been wrong. I was also willing to admit that even if he had made a mistake, I had certainly made my share, too. There were so many things I wanted to say, so many things I knew I should say. And someday I would. I hoped. I was still a work in progress, so while I wasn't quite ready to have that conversation, I now understood in the blink of an eye, a slip in the shower, a drunk at an intersection, or a bus in the dark, he could be gone and I would never have the chance. I reached up and hooked an arm around his neck, pulled him down, and kissed him full on the mouth. At the moment, I think it said more than words could have.

"I'll do my best." He smiled and his eyes were warm and maybe a little hopeful when they met mine. Maybe he did know me pretty well, after all. "Do you think I could email you while I'm gone? You know, just to make sure Dirk isn't horning in on my practice. I'm sure service will be spotty so no guarantees. Is your email still MadMax@aol.com?"

"Yeah, it is." I laughed. I wasn't looking for guarantees. I knew now there weren't any.

****

Gail looked at least ten years younger once she learned she didn't have a terminal illness. Dad had obviously been shaken by the whole ordeal since he even agreed to leave the store in the capable hands of his assistant manager and actually take a day off to bring his wife home. I think it was a first.

I decided a traditional Logan family Sunday coffee klatch didn't have to wait until Sunday, mid-week worked just fine. Since Dad would be at the hospital to retrieve Gail, and Denise wouldn't be over until later in the morning with the twins, I planned to get up early, head to the bakery, make a pit stop at the SuperSave, and have everything set up and waiting at the house. I pulled my tee over my head and stepped under my Chastings Corque Corian Square Ceiling Mount Showerhead. Strangely, I didn't think of Tarzan even once. I poured a handful of strawberry shampoo into my hands and began to lather, rinse, and repeat. It was a minute before I realized something was wrong, very wrong. Impossibly, the back of my head was whole and intact. No gash, no staples, no blood-matted hair. What the hell?

Another Christmas miracle? Oh, wait, it was still June. I rinsed off quickly, not even bothering to shave my legs, and dried off even faster. I looked in the mirror, ran my fingers all through my hair, and even knocked my head off of the wall a few times, but the staples were gone. Huh. Maybe it had something to do with the fact I wasn't supposed to have died in the first place and now I'd lived up to my end of the bargain, I was healed?

Huh.

I dumped a can of food into Caesar's dish—need I reiterate he remained unimpressed?—and then I ran down to my car. The eco-tote, two empty water bottles, and the four pack of toilet paper were still in the back seat. I vowed I absolutely would clean the car this weekend.

After a nearly traffic free drive downtown—I mean who is out driving around at nine on a Wednesday morning—I made a quick stop at the bakery for bagels and Long Johns, and then slid into a slot in the SuperSave parking lot. I was only mildly surprised to see Buddy back working the checkout. I guessed his suspension got rescinded when my term as temporary

SSI came to an end. For his sake, and Marvin's nerves, I hoped he would straighten up and go by the book from now on. I flew through the dairy aisle, the plastic basket slung over my arm. I loaded in some Half and Half and cream cheese, then added a package of Break-N-Bake cinnamon rolls purely because I was feeling festive. Of course, I got in Buddy's line. I mean, I thought he might want to apologize for killing me and all, and I was feeling a little sorry I'd gotten him in trouble.

There was only one person ahead of me and soon Buddy was scanning my items as if he was any other normal high school kid working at a summer job. When he finished with my pitifully few items he eyed me politely over the top of his Coke bottle-thick Buddy Holly specs, one grimy-nailed finger poised over the register key.

"Will that be all, ma'am?"

"Cut the crap, Buddy, it's me," I whispered.

"Excuse me?" he said, looking genuinely puzzled. I was not amused.

"Okay, you want to play that game? Fine by me. I basically wanted to say I was sorry for having you suspended. Of course, considering you killed me, I'm sure you understand I was a little upset at the time."

"Uh, lady, are you okay?" I saw Buddy gesture discreetly to someone behind me. I almost fainted when I spun on my heel and found myself face to coffee stained tie and heroically straining buttons with Bob Grubly.

"Bob, oh my God, what are you doing here?" I nearly screamed. Were things so tight at the Grubly house the man couldn't even afford to take a few days off to mourn his wife? There had to be some law against that somewhere. I would find out, I would make sure they gave Bob whatever time he needed, I would…

"I work here, Max," Bob said slowly. *When speaking to children use small words and enunciate.* "You know that. Are you okay?"

"Well, sure I'm okay, Bob. But, what about you? I mean, Gerri…" I trailed off lamely. I didn't know what to say.

"Oh, well…yeah, I know I said I didn't want her working, but now she got that job at the Curl Up and Dye, she seems really happy. And the extra money sure does help. I guess I was being a little unreasonable. I'm just an old fashioned guy like that, I suppose." Bob smiled sheepishly.

"So, Gerri…she's okay?" I breathed, hardly daring to believe it. The Curl Up and Dye? Seriously?

"Sure, she's swell," Bob gave me a perplexed look. For the record, swell ranks right up there with gee whiz in my book, but I had recently developed a new-found fondness for Bob which allowed me to overlook it.

"Oh, ah…okay, that's great, Bob, beyond great. In fact, you have no idea *how* great. I am *so* happy to hear that, you can't even *imagine* how happy I am. Tell her I said hi, okay?" I couldn't help myself. I stretched my arms around Bob's enormous girth and gave him a big, heartfelt hug. I must admit he looked a little taken aback by my unexpected enthusiasm for his wife's well-being, but he took it like a man.

Bob and Buddy were both looking at me like my elevator wasn't going all the way to the top floor. I grabbed my eco-tote and continued to smile brightly with a look that probably bordered on maniacal as I made my way through the line and toward the door. They continued to stare after me as though deciding whether they should wave goodbye or call the men in the little white coats. I knew it wasn't all a dream, it couldn't have all been a dream...could it? But it must have been. There was no other explanation.

I was so preoccupied, I failed to negotiate the elderly woman loading her twenty seven bags of canned cat food into her cart at the end of the next line. We both escaped injury free, but I dropped my eco-tote and the contents spilled all over the floor. As I grabbed the handle and started to shove everything back inside, I saw a familiar small, brown book mixed in with my Half and Half, cream cheese, and Break-N-Bakes. I opened the cover, and there it was.

Life and Death are much the same.
Neither comes with an instruction manual.
Nicely done. Enjoy your reward.
                    M.

I caught my breath and looked up. Buddy and Bob were still staring at me. Bob remained slightly confounded, but Buddy smiled his purple braced grin.

My reward? What in the name of marshmallow fluff did Marvin mean? Then it hit me.

"Gerri?" I whispered. But, how could that even be possible? Of course, if I learned anything over the last few days, it was that the borders surrounding possibility extended far beyond anything I ever hoped to understand. Again, I glanced at Buddy. And the little weasel winked.

Epilogue

Thankfully, Roger survived Somalia and arrived home last week, thinner but happier. His emails were few and far between, filled with wonder and a passion for his work and the people he met there, which I'm not sure he could have found anywhere else. I have an uneasy feeling the humanitarian mission thing could become a recurrent event. I guess I'll learn to deal with it if and when the time comes.

Gail is happy and healthy, her blood counts holding steady, and after I select a few things of my mom's I really want to keep, she, Denise, and I are going to redecorate my apartment. It isn't my idea, but it gives them a cheap thrill so I'm trying to go with the flow. Roger has agreed to take Caesar for the duration—Gail going into anaphylactic shock would kind of put a damper on the whole project. Denise insists it's my Christmas in July present. I told her I will be paying, but she is free to accessorize.

Speaking of paying, I actually have a non-alimony related income these days. I'm working at Logan's Hardware. It's not a lifetime career choice, at least I don't think it is, but it does free Dad up to take some time off. He seems to feel as long as there is a family member behind the counter, the place is in good hands, even if they're mine. The blue denim work apron isn't exactly a fashion statement, but at least it isn't red polyester.

A group of nurses at Beaumont South got together and filed a grievance charging Dirk Kramer with creating a hostile work environment and sexual harassment. He, of course, is denying everything, but I heard he has expressed an interest in moving his practice, and his cask of cologne, to New Jersey.

Roger and I have a date this week. We're going to Alberto's for Spaghetti alla Carbonara. After much persuasion, and a little groveling on my part, Alberto has agreed to give me a second chance. He's Italian, he understands passion. It seems I've been given a lot of second chances lately. Maybe they were always there and I never recognized them, or maybe I lacked the courage to embrace them. I think the more important thing is I've learned to give them, and realize you can't live your life taking them for granted. Not everything comes with a do-over. Once you burn a bridge, you probably shouldn't try to repair it because it's never as strong as it once was, and in the end, it just might burn faster. But, that doesn't mean you can't recycle some of the wood to try to build a new one.

I heard a song once that said, *the past is gone, but something might be found to take its place.* And so I'm trying. And I've learned to let others try, too. Sometimes it's not what you do, but what you don't do that hurts other people the most. I don't claim I've become the person I should be. Heck, I haven't even managed to become the person I hope to be. But, I'm definitely not the person I was. And that's a good thing. I think. This is not to say I don't still sometimes believe tact is for people who aren't smart enough for sarcasm. There are still many, many days I wish karma worked instantaneously. Forgiving doesn't mean forgetting, it simply means you learn to handle your life without letting the past kick you in the face on a daily basis.

Life isn't easy or fair. Life lessons are hard and you can't study, cheat, or copy off of the guy sitting next to you. You can't Google them or find them on Wikipedia. I know, I checked. I don't care what Alicia says, that little brown book of Marvin's is no help at all. But, she was right about one thing—you can't control what happens, but you can choose how you respond. I believe now that everything happens for a reason.

Well, except for clowns. I mean, seriously? And black socks with sandals. Yeah, we're still working on that.

I finally understand I can still be happy when everything isn't going my way, and people don't have to be perfect in order for me to love them. Let's face it, if common sense was an explosive, some people wouldn't have enough to make a decent firecracker. But that's just the way it is. And the real gift is I don't have to be perfect in order for people to love me, either. I disappoint people despite my best intentions, and that's okay because they disappoint me, too. Falling down is a part of life. Getting back up and forcing yourself to keep moving forward until you get beyond the obstacle is living.

Was my brief tenure as the Superintendent of Supernatural Interventions real, or merely a bizarre dream brought on a by an up close and personal encounter with Italian marble?

Not. A. Clue.

And ultimately whether I actually died or not, Death taught me that it really is all about me, only not in the way I thought. So, my unsolicited opinion?

Yeah, I know you didn't ask for it, no one ever does. That's why it's called unsolicited.

Someday I hope you get the chance to live as if you died. I think everyone will agree Eleanor Roosevelt may not have been the most attractive first lady this country has ever had, but she knew her stuff. She said that no one can make you feel inferior without your consent. Sometimes, without ever even realizing it, you become your own worst enemy. So, whatever comes your way? Get over it. Put on your big girl panties and pull them up.

Like frozen bagels...life comes with an expiration date.

A word about the author...

Sharon Saracino was born and raised in the anthracite coal region of Pennsylvania and resides there with her long suffering husband, funny and talented son, and two insane dogs. She believes that all roads lead to happily ever after, some just have a few unexpected turns! When she is not reading, writing, or formulating a plan to get an extra day added to the weekend, she brews limoncello, dreams of moving to Italy, and works as a Certified Registered Rehabilitation Nurse.

http://sharonsaracino.com

www.ingramcontent.com/pod-product-compliance
Lightning Source LLC
Chambersburg PA
CBHW060934180626
46817CB00004B/1530